CW00473908

SMALL LIVES, BIG WORLD

A Collection of Short Stories from Near and Far

R.M. GREEN

Copyright © 2016 R. M. Green

The moral right of the author has been asserted.

Apart from any fair dealing for the purposes of research or private study,
or criticism or review, as permitted under the Copyright, Designs and Patents
Act 1988, this publication may only be reproduced, stored or transmitted, in
any form or by any means, with the prior permission in writing of the
publishers, or in the case of reprographic reproduction in accordance with
the terms of licences issued by the Copyright Licensing Agency. Enquiries
concerning reproduction outside those terms should be sent to the publishers.

This is a work of fiction. Names, characters, businesses, places, events
and incidents are either the products of the author's imagination
or used in a fictitious manner. Any resemblance to actual persons,
living or dead, or actual events is purely coincidental.

Matador
9 Priory Business Park,
Wistow Road, Kibworth Beauchamp,
Leicestershire. LE8 0RX
Tel: 0116 279 2299
Email: books@troubador.co.uk
Web: www.troubador.co.uk/matador
Twitter: @matadorbooks

ISBN 978 1785890 277

British Library Cataloguing in Publication Data.
A catalogue record for this book is available from the British Library.

Printed and bound in the UK by TJ International, Padstow, Cornwall
Typeset in 11pt Aldine401 BT by Troubador Publishing Ltd, Leicester, UK

Matador is an imprint of Troubador Publishing Ltd

This book is dedicated to Dominic and to the memory of Yelena;
the very best of people.

And for my mum, Pauline 1934-2015, a legend.

CONTENTS

FOREWORD

Having travelled extensively and lived in countries foreign to the land of my birth for the majority of my adult life, I have been fortunate enough to have experienced much. Although the environments and cultures may differ wildly, the commonality of the human condition is indeed, universal. That much is obvious. My stories are largely that; different ingredients with different flavours perhaps, but we all eat at the same table!

The vast majority of us lead small, decent lives and all of us are confronted, now and again, with extraordinary situations. Some see us flourish, others see us fail, but I have noticed that our capacity for hope is the one thing that unites people of faith or of no faith when faced with adversity.

It is my hope that these few stories reflect that.

THE INTERVIEW

The two men sat across the small waiting area studiously avoiding looking at each other directly but stealing glances every now and then, weighing each other up, judging each other, resenting each other, despising each other. A year ago, maybe more, they might have struck up a conversation, found mutual ground, solidarity in adversity and empathy. But now, like prize-fighters waiting for the bell for the last round, they were too wary, too exhausted, with too much at stake for friendship. It was horribly gladiatorial. One would triumph; one would limp from the field, vanquished. Both knew it. Had they both been in their twenties, it would all have seemed as a game; win some, lose some, c'est la vie and all that. But the wrong side of forty-five, this was, so they felt, their last chance. Only one of them would feel the joy. No, no longer the joy, merely intense relief. The other would be plunged once more into that bitter pit of failure, perhaps for the final time, never again to crawl out. The dry tongues behind clenched teeth articulated the same silent prayer, *Please let it be me. Please let it be me.*

"If you would be so kind as to wait," they said. "We will call you back in after our deliberations. Help yourselves to coffee from the machine. We'll be with you as soon as possible. So kind." That was almost thirty minutes ago. It was barbaric. White-collar torture. Slow death by polystyrene cup of decaffeinated sludge, three-year-old trade magazines and the excruciating tick of the white-faced clock on the wall.

It was hot and suffocating and the fan in the corner was so weak that all it managed was to disturb the heavy air directly in front of it, offering no relief from the oppression of the August afternoon. Despite this, both men kept their suit jackets on; the slightly heavier set man, to hide the dark patches of sweat he knew would be forming soup plate-sized discs under his arms and spreading like a wet rash over his back, the other, more slender and hungry-looking, to cover up a recently acquired curry stain on his one good silk tie.

Whoever they call in first, it'll be to tell them the bad news. Get that out the way, then call in the winner. That's how it goes, thought Peter.

They will want to get the unpleasantness over first then get down to business, Graham mused.

It was unusual. The final two candidates called to a decisive interview at the same time. They had explained that the factory was to shut down for two weeks for the summer holidays and that the management wanted to make a decision today. They were strong candidates and it was felt only fair to ask them both in as the divisional manager, Nigel, was only available this afternoon as he was going off to Crete that evening. So here they were, the select duo, the favoured pair, stewing in the stale, airless waiting area while their fate was being decided behind a white gloss-painted door. Peter had arrived while Graham was inside. Asked by the bored receptionist to make his way upstairs and take a seat, he had waited for fifteen minutes distractedly working on a crossword puzzle in the *Metro* newspaper. When Graham came out, Peter had stood up and his focus was on the young woman he recognised from his first interview a week before. He hardly noticed the other man who went over to the coffee machine, and with a brief handshake, the woman, whose name he had forgotten and who didn't re-introduce herself, ushered him into the room with a, "Nice to see you again. This way please." Twenty minutes or so later, Peter emerged, also headed for the coffee machine, poured himself a cup, resumed his seat and took up his paper once more. The two men were seated opposite each other separated by just a few feet of threadbare carpet and a chrome-framed table with a smoky glass top decorated with perfectly circular rings of long-dried coffee. The table was strewn with old magazines, a blue board marker missing its cap, several empty thimble-size pots of UHT milk, carelessly scattered torn sachets of sugar with a powdering of crystals and plastic stirrers, and, curiously enough, a desk calendar (showing the month of April 2013) in Japanese with a photograph of St Basil's Cathedral in Moscow on it. So they sat, silent and mutually unacknowledged. And sat. And sat.

A single rivulet of sweat meandered down Graham's temple, slightly stinging his eye as he flicked unseeingly through *Marketing Today*, March 2014. Across the faded biscuit-brown carpet, Peter's back was drenched in perspiration and he shifted forward in his chair then back again feeling the damp coolness against his skin, clammy and unpleasant. From over his copy of the *Metro*, his watery-brown eyes glanced surreptitiously for the hundredth time across the room as he contemplated his balding adversary; this crumpled nemesis in a blue M&S wool and polyester double-breasted suit. And suddenly, Peter wanted to cry. A sob of desperation welled up in his chest and he suppressed it just before it escaped his lips as a heart-wrenching keen. He felt sick. He coughed in an attempt to gain control over himself and looked quickly back to his paper as this drew the attention of the other man who darted a glance over at the sound. Graham had nervously looked up as a reflex drew him to the source of the noise and only just avoided eye contact as the other man hurriedly threw his attention back to his newspaper.

Graham was nauseous and swallowed repeatedly. His mouth was dry and in an effort to generate some saliva he set down the magazine on the cluttered table and picking up his cup, flicked his tongue inside to glean the last cold drop of brown liquid, biting into the polystyrene as he did so. Swallowing again, he contemplated the crooked indentation of his teeth on the cup, then, suddenly embarrassed by this juvenile display, he leant forward and without getting up, tossed the cup into the green metal wastepaper bin behind the door. The other man was still engrossed in the ten-times-read paper and Graham's movement appeared to have gone unnoticed.

Sitting back in his chair and self-consciously patting his jacket front which concealed the curry-stained tie, Graham slyly studied the man across the room in detail. Pale-skinned with a yellowish tinge, a heavy smoker no doubt. The man looked around fifty and had dark brown hair flecked with grey, cropped close to his round head. His eyes were the colour of dirty dishwater, washed out greyish-brown, and the whites were also tinged with yellow. He was clean-shaven but in the heat of the afternoon his jaw glistened with light sweat and showed the beginnings of stubble which gave him a slightly sordid appearance. His shirt was pale blue and Graham noticed it was darker around the edge of the collar. He felt rather pleased that he had chosen a white shirt on such a sweltering day, although again, was pricked by a stab of shame at his lamb madras-blotted tie. The suit, plain grey and although now a little creased, was obviously a very good one, and Graham couldn't help but look at it with an envious yet spiteful gaze. He gained some cold comfort from the obvious sweat marks on the shirt; the unsuitability of the blue tie with rather loud yellow spots; and the inch of skin exposed between the cuffed trousers and the top of the grey socks as the man sat with his legs crossed at the ankles. His black Italian shoes were obviously new and looked like they must have pinched his swollen feet in this heat. *Good!* Graham thought uncharitably. Then he remembered the hole in his polished but well-worn C&A lace-ups and planted his feet more squarely on the carpet.

He felt guilty. He didn't really mean this chap any harm. It's just that he stood between Graham and probably his last chance and he hated him for it. He hated himself for feeling so desperate and above all, he hated those kids inside, currently deciding his fate. The three of them all looked younger than his daughter: so confident and casual, so damn patronising, so necessary for his future. Pitiful. Grovelling and abasing himself, obsequiously humble, telling them whatever they wanted to hear. And for what? Thirty grand and private healthcare to. do a job he had been doing before these kids were out of Pampers. *How did I get to this?* he asked himself morosely, self-pityingly. He knew the answer. Ten years ago he was a company director. He worked hard and enjoyed it mostly. But he drank a bit. Then Susan left him when Daisy went to university. She said she never really loved him and that now, without Daisy at home, she wanted more from life than ironing his shirts and rolling him into bed after another boozy dinner with customers. She was going back to university herself, as a mature student and to find her true self. Her true self! Bitch! Graham knew that she was carrying on with that bloke, Jim, from her amateur dramatics group. But he said nothing. He watched her go. The divorce was the easy bit. He got the house and the timeshare in Florida. She got the cash and the shares and the few antiques. He was earning a decent amount and soon he met Grace. It was his forty-fourth birthday; work laid on a surprise party to cheer him up and she was actually *in* the cake:

a big-breasted, false blonde, over-the-hill stripper with stretch marks and protruding front teeth. They hit it off immediately. She, sitting heavily on his lap pouring Asti down his throat he, embarrassed but aroused and she could feel it.

After that first meeting, when he got her number, they went out a few times. Dinner and drinks, a lot of drinks. They matched each other glass for glass, bitter memory for bitter memory. She moved in after his divorce. Her boy, Darren, was in the army and never contacted her. Darren's father had left eighteen years before having tried his best to beat the foetus out of her. "Damaged goods, sweetie. That's what I am," she laughed as she threw back another glass. Vodka was their tipple. They were happy in their alcoholic stupor and Graham thought it would go on that way until he retired. Then he would sell the timeshare and buy a place in the sun outright, maybe there in Florida, maybe Spain, and they would live drunkenly ever after.

Then Grace got ill: kidney failure. Dialysis three times a week. Graham realised how much he really loved her. He stopped drinking. He sold the timeshare and with the proceeds bought a dialysis machine. He took care of Grace and she cried because no one had ever cared for her that much. He lost his job. Too much time off work. That was four years ago. They had moved into a small flat. The money from the sale of the house helped them get by for a while but it was running low and no transplant was in sight. He had to get another

7

job. He had been looking for over a year now. Sending his CV in to all and sundry. Interview after interview but at his age, they explained, even with senior executive experience, the opportunities are just not there. "So sorry." Perhaps, if he were willing to retrain, to take a more junior position? So, it had come to this. Sitting in this black hole of Calcutta, dripping with sweat, wearing a stained tie and wishing the bloke opposite you, a perfect stranger, would drop dead so that he would be left clear to become the Thomas Electrical, Spares Division Sales Executive (South) reporting to the Spares Division Sales Manager (UK) who had more acne than skin on his face and who had called him 'Gray'. He closed his eyes as another wave of nausea crashed over him. Then he thought of Grace and why he was doing this and it made it all bearable. Poor Gracie. He opened his eyes as the door suddenly opened and another young woman, this one, very attractive with an impressive Afro, wearing designer jeans flared at the bottom and a plain white cotton blouse which resembled a Russian peasant-smock stepped not entirely over the threshold. Both men jumped up. Both silently cursed their lack of control as they did so: too damn eager, too bloody desperate.

"Mr Smithson, Mr Parsons, sorry to keep you," said the woman addressing both yet looking at neither of them but with a sweet smile and a note of genuine contrition in her voice which had the softest of Jamaican accents. "We just need a few more minutes. We are waiting on a conference call with head office. Help yourselves to more coffee," she said, nodding in the direction of the coffee machine in the corner in which was left nothing but bitter dregs. Then just as quickly as she had appeared, the woman disappeared and the white gloss-painted door was shut in their faces. Without acknowledging each other, both men resumed their seats.

The relentless ticking from the white-faced clock, the pathetic whine of the useless fan and the odd residual burble from the coffee machine were, once again, the main soundtrack to this purgatorial scene. The window was open but the air was too still to provide any relief to the leaden atmosphere and even the dull hum of distant traffic seemed to add to the oppression. From behind the door a phone rang twice and faint and indistinct murmurings could be heard from within.

Can't be much longer now. God, I could do with a fag, thought Peter to himself as he strained to hear, in vain, the muffled voices on the other side of the door.

The diffused light of the sun, broken up by the skeletal shadows cast by the metal window frame, flooded the room yet somehow did not make it brighter. It was a lazy, yellow light that made the pale green walls look more like the colour of freshly spewed baby food than anything else. Peter felt his stomach churn and tried to calm himself by focusing on the man opposite him who was sitting erect with his head leant back and his eyes closed. Although he had spent a good deal of time observing the man, Peter couldn't remember what colour his eyes were. Blue, perhaps. He looked down at his sleeve and removed an invisible piece of lint. He liked this suit: grey light wool, tailor-made for him when he was at Bradley's Far East Office in Hong Kong. He sighed. So long ago. He looked back across at the other man and contemptuously dismissed his cheap blue suit, but remarked to himself that the burnt-crimson silk tie did, indeed, look very fine. The man was sweating much less than he was and although his bald forehead, surrounded with thin sandy hair, was pricked with beads of perspiration, he seemed altogether less wrung out than Peter felt.

Shifting uncomfortably in his seat, Peter gave up trying to decipher the voices behind the door and wondered if he would really do what he was contemplating if this job didn't work out. It didn't bear thinking about. He was fifty-three. Fifteen years ago he was head of purchasing for Bradley's, a large importer of cheap household electronics made in the Far East. He had a small but plush office in Hong Kong, a company penthouse, a maid, a generous expat salary and a somewhat carefree lifestyle. He was what the papers used to call 'a confirmed bachelor' and in fact, he preferred this term to openly coming out as gay. He was discreet and monogamous, and his partner, an Australian flight attendant called Stanley who worked for Cathay Pacific, was the love of his life. Then in the space of three weeks, it all came crashing down. Bradley's sold out to a Chinese conglomerate and Peter was given a generous pay off but only three weeks to clear out of his apartment. When Stanley heard that the penthouse and expat lifestyle were to be taken away, leaving just Peter, he requested a change of route from the airline and walked out. Peter returned to Britain hurt, confused and alone.

He had been away from Britain for too long. All his old contacts had moved on. He knew no one and England seemed an alien country to him. He had his generous redundancy so he rented rooms in Chelsea and set about looking for a job. He was not wealthy enough to retire and he needed to work for his own sanity. Stanley had broken his heart and he knew that if he couldn't throw himself into work, he would go under. For three years he tried everything and all the time he grew older and even less employable. The last time he saw the recruitment consultant, he had been told that it might be best for him to set his targets lower and to look for something part-time. The DIY places are always looking for mature, reliable staff. Why not try there? That had almost killed him. He developed an ulcer and was on sleeping pills prescribed by an overworked and disinterested GP. So now, he was faced with the choice of taking his dwindling savings and eking out his early old age in a grotty flat in Battersea, or taking any job that came along. This one was his last chance. After hundreds of rejections, Peter had no self-respect left. If he didn't get this, he was not going to sacrifice the very last shred of his dignity and rot in a bedsit. He had made up his mind. This time, if he lost out again, he would check into the best room in the Grosvenor Hotel with a full bottle of Jonny Walker Blue Label, an equally full bottle of sleeping pills and after a luxurious shower, he would sit in his Chinese silk dressing gown with Stravinsky on the CD player. After a meal of caviar followed by half a dozen oysters and Dover sole, Peter would wash down the entire bottle of pills with the whisky and sod the lot of them.

Yet he knew. He knew by his profuse sweating, which was more than just because of the heat; he knew by his hostile resentment of the stranger opposite; by his straining to catch every decipherable syllable from the next room that he wanted to live, wanted to work, wanted to be. But he also knew he hadn't the strength left to try again if it ended this time as it had done so often in the last three years.

Then they heard the door being opened. For the first time both men looked at each other and there, in that instant, they bonded. All was forgiven and each felt the other's pain and hope. They were brothers.

The sweet, smiling, confident young woman with the large Afro stepped into the room.

"Mr Parsons?" she asked in a friendly voice.

TIME IS RELATIVE

There was something deeply satisfying in the click of the electric platform clock as it registered the passing of another minute. Another minute closer to the train's arrival.

12:16

The screen showed that the 12:46 to Edinburgh via Doncaster and York was expected at its appointed hour. Just another thirty minutes and then he would be on the way back to the city he hadn't seen in fifty years. He closed his eyes and was walking along Princes Street – a young man in a tweed jacket, Brylcreem and brogues.

"Thirty more minutes! Oh no! That's like, forever! ...Granddad, how long *is* thirty minutes?"

The old man was shaken from his reverie by the eager, fidgety six-year-old tugging at his sleeve.

"What's that? Thirty minutes. Why, it's the tiniest time! When Mummy takes you to school in the car, I bet that's much longer than thirty minutes. When you are older, thirty minutes will be a quick as a sneeze – Atchoo!"

"How old will I be then, Granddad?"

"When?"

"When I'm older? Will I be as old as you?"

"And how old do you think I am?"

"Oh like, really old!"

The child started counting on his mittened fingers. Holding up both hands, fingers splayed he said, "You are really old – thirty-five? Yes," he declared, "you are thirty-five… That's old isn't it, Granddad?"

The old man smiled, "Yes, that is really old, but I am even older. I am older than you can count!"

"Wow!" exclaimed the boy staring in open-mouthed wonder at his superannuated grandparent.

A work crew strolled along the tracks. The boy waved at them and the men waved back.

12:24

Together they watched in silence as a freight train clacked and creaked, scraped and whined, clanged and rattled its way through the station.

"Granddad… Ben says that when we get old, we die, like Ben's rabbit. He was only four but Ben says that's really old for a rabbit because they are small. His dad planted it in the garden like a tree. When you die, will Daddy plant you in the garden too?"

"Well, I may be old, but I don't think I would make a very good tree, so I won't die just yet."

"Good. I don't want you to be a tree."

12:32

"Granddad, thirty minutes is nearly over now, isn't it?"

"Yes. See, I told you it was the tiniest time!"

"So how long will the train take to go to Edingbug?"

"Edinburgh."

"Yes, how long will it take to go to Edingbug?"

"About two and a half hours."

"Two and a half hours! …Granddad, is two and a half hours a long time?"

The platform clock blinked and 12:35 gave way to 12:36. A few notes on a pre-recorded glockenspiel and a muffled announcement prevented any immediate reply from the old man. The train slid into the station – noiselessly to the old man, nothing like the hissing, chugging, smoke-belching steam locomotives of his salad days – ear-splittingly loudly to the child, just like a spaceship.

"On a train, two and a half hours is like thirty minutes when you are standing still. There is so much to see – trees, fields, cows, horses, towns and villages. You won't even notice the time."

"Well, I want to live on a train so I can grow up quicker and drive Daddy's car!"

They settled into their seats and both the boy and his grandfather looked excitedly out of the window. After twenty minutes, the old man drifted off somewhere between sleep and memory. The little boy yawned, put

15

his head on the armrest and clutching his grandfather's coat, he fell asleep.

They both slept until the guard gently woke them at Waverley Station.

THE CHRISTMAS CARD

The following story was inspired by an item appearing on the
BBC News website on Thursday 15th February 2007.

A postcard sent from the trenches in World War
One has just been delivered – 90 years late.
Soldier Walter Butler was eighteen and fighting in
the trenches in France when he sent the card to his
fiancée, Amy Hicks, in Colerne, Wiltshire.

Walter knew he was going to die. The thought of his
imminent death held no fear for him. He had faced it so
often and seen so much of it in the past few months in
this featureless Flanders wasteland that the prospect of
dying neither surprised nor terrified him.

If anything, he felt a dark sense of irony. For what
was killing him weren't the bullets of the Germans, nor
the mustard gas, nor the cold steel of an unrelenting
bayonet that had done for so many of his mates in the
trenches. Nor was it the murderous cold or the disease
that riddled this underfed, poorly clothed, disastrously
led, rabble of human cannon-fodder; the wilted flower
of a generation sacrificed to the caprice and useless pride
of a handful of European royal cousins. It was a biscuit
box that had done it for Walter. Foraging for food for

himself and a wounded comrade among the putrid body parts in the bottom of a trench slick with mud, blood and human waste, Walter had cut his hand open on the jagged edge of an empty biscuit tin. He was so caked in filth and slime, he barely noticed. When he clambered back into the rotting wooden shelter that passed as a staging post for wounded soldiers waiting for the stretcher-bearers to pick them up and carry them back a few hundred yards behind the lines to the butcher's yard that was laughingly called a field hospital, Walter found that his mate, Billy, was dead. At eighteen and a half, he was two weeks younger than Walter.

"Poor sod. But just as well," he thought grimly. Billy had been blinded by a grenade and had lost an arm. Death was a mercy. It was also a mercy for the stretcher-bearers, the bravest men in the army, who could postpone their next foray for a little while. Unarmed, they often faced the fury of the battle to ferry the dead and dying away from the killing fields. People always talked about the three-week average life expectancy of a pilot. The life of a stretcher-bearer was often half that.

It was late November 1916. Walter didn't even really know where he was. It all looked the same anyway. It was just mile upon mile of flat, barbed wire-strewn, half-frozen mud, and so cold that Walter felt no pain in his hand. He was so filthy that he paid scant attention to the blood clotted in his palm. It had been weeks since he could feel his fingers anyway. Ten days after he had cut himself, Walter lay on a flea-infested mattress, in a field hospital, shivering under a threadbare horse blanket, drifting in and out of occasionally delirious consciousness, half aware of the dull thud and boom of distant artillery. The young Scottish nurse held his trembling hand and caressed him with soothing words; she reminded him of Amy in that she was everything this war was not: kind, gentle and soft. Such kindness after such brutality was almost more than Walter could bear. He sent her away to find him a pen and an army issue regimental postcard. He wanted to send Amy a Christmas card, to let her know that he loved her while he still had a little time. The blood poisoning was in an advanced stage and the young lieutenant doctor, another Scot called Calder from Sutherland – barely older than Walter himself who had been in the third year of his medical studies at the University of Edinburgh when he was called up – could do nothing. Even if he could have helped, he had no drugs; nothing to ease the pain. They had run out of morphine months ago. He was 23 but he looked 50. Two years later, the week after Armistice, Hamish Calder would take his service revolver, which he had never drawn before, and put a bullet in his brain.

Walter barely had the strength to write and even then he had to do so with his left hand as they had amputated the right hand in a vain attempt to stop the spread of the poisoning. The nurse propped his head up on the ragged remains of his greatcoat and holding his hand in hers helped him write on the card, which was regulation ivory-white and bore a small ribbon of blue and red in the regimental colours and a sketch of a cheerful sprig of holly for decoration. There were tears in both their eyes as they wrote:

'My dearest Amy,

A very Merry Christmas to you and your family. I will be home soon, so don't cry and be the brave, lovely girl that I know you to be.

Your ever loving, Walter.'

There was neither the space, nor the strength for any more. As the nurse finished writing the address which Walter dictated to her, she thought of this poor girl back in a little farm cottage in Wiltshire, and how she would never see her beau again, and a tear spilled onto the card, smudging the date, 10th December 1916. She dried her eyes and went to make her patient more comfortable. But Walter was now beyond the pain, beyond the trenches, beyond the misery. She closed his unseeing eyes and took the postcard to give to the regimental dispatch while the orderlies took the body from the bed because there were others who needed it now.

Back at the little cottage on the farm in Wiltshire, Amy had no idea that Walter would never be coming home to marry her. She sat by the fire, knitting a little blanket, her plump silhouette flickering on the stone wall behind her. When Walter, looking so handsome and full of life, had proposed on his last day on the farm before going off to training camp, Amy hadn't hesitated. They had been sweethearts since Miss Gordon's class in the village school when they were six years old. They had gone for a walk and on that balmy late April afternoon, when he had asked and she had joyously agreed with tears in her eyes; they went hand in hand into the little spinney down by the river and had tenderly, if a little clumsily, made love for the first and only time in their young lives. When she discovered she was pregnant, her parents were dismayed but not overly angry. Things like that tended to happen more often in the country, especially in wartime, her mother had explained. Amy wasn't sure whether she believed her mother but there was no scandal. After all, everyone in the village knew that she and Walter were to be married and it was only natural what with him going off to war. Amy didn't know for certain but she thought that it would be different in a big city like Salisbury. In any event, she decided not to tell Walter in her letters because she didn't want him to worry about her and not look after himself as he ought. The baby, a little girl, was born in January 1917. Two weeks later, Walter's father called at the cottage to see his granddaughter 'for the third time this week', laughing at the gruff yet good-natured ploughman's pride in his new kin. But he just stood at the threshold, wordless, clutching a piece of

21

paper in his trembling, hoary hands. Amy knew what it was immediately. Everybody always knew. It was Army Form B. 104-82 from the War Office.

★★★

Wendy Pennington yawned, stirred her coffee as quietly as she could and tried to will away her splitting headache and suppress the wave of nausea that was surging within her.

"Another day, another hangover," she murmured bitterly in a hoarse whisper. As she tried to sip the coffee as delicately as possible, Wendy contemplated her relatively new surroundings with little of the excitement she had hoped and longed for.

It was five days before Christmas, her forty-somethingth birthday and her first weekend in the cottage. She had started as head of the art department at the local secondary school at the beginning of the academic year that September, and had been living as a reluctant flatmate with an equally reluctant host, a geography teacher called Simon who hated company but needed the rent, until the sale of the cottage went through.

Groaning slightly, Wendy went to one of the many still-to-be-unpacked cardboard boxes in the corner of the kitchen to search with rather more hope than expectation for some aspirin. Returning to her chair empty-handed, she surveyed the remains of her previous evening's supper; a large bowl of pasta with butter and half a tub of vanilla ice-cream, straight from the tub. She had used the same fork for both. There was also an empty bottle of red Bordeaux and an almost empty mug containing the flotsam of a used teabag and several cigarette ends. A crushed packet of Silk Cut, a yellow plastic lighter and an open laptop computer on stand-by mode completed the scene. Wendy sighed and coughed and tried not to feel as bedraggled and dire as she thought she must look.

Gingerly taking another sip of her coffee, Wendy pressed a key and the laptop screen flickered into life and welcomed her by name. Tapping another few keys with one finger, Wendy checked her inbox. There were three new messages and all of them wishing her a happy birthday – one from her car insurer, another from a gym in Southend, which she had joined three years ago and had attended precisely once thereafter, and the third from her mother:

"Dear Gwendolyn,

Wishing you many happy returns and season's greetings and that you finally find your direction in life,

Mother."

Not, 'love, Mum' or anything so warm. She even combined the 'happy birthday' with the 'Merry Christmas' in the driest fashion. It had been the same

23

thing with her combined birthday and Christmas present as a little girl. The one thing that cheered Wendy up was knowing how much her mother would hate to be reminded that her daughter was well over forty years old! Miserable cow! It was bad enough she had saddled her daughter with the absurd name of Gwendolyn and made her early years an affectionless wasteland, but now she had the barefaced cheek to criticise her whenever she made, thankfully rare, contact. *No wonder Dad buggered off with that cruise ship*, Wendy thought. She couldn't blame her dad. He had borne the full brunt of the chilled bitterness from his wife as long as possible and then one day when Wendy was ten had given her a big hug, twenty pounds and told her he was, "Right sorry, Petal, but she'll be the bloody death of me." He left as a Steward with P&O and had kept in touch regularly, right up to his death three years ago in his whitewashed bungalow in the Algarve. It was the money from the sale of this 'little sun-soaked villa', as he was fond of calling it, which had substantially paid for the cottage.

As soon as Wendy had done her A levels, she left her mother to her Edwardian terraced townhouse in Cheltenham and her several elderly lodgers, and went to Oxford Polytechnic to study art with vague dreams of becoming a fabulous sculptress, notorious for wild parties with the sort of bright young things from the gossip columns. However, Wendy was a diligent but limited artist, allergic to marijuana and wasn't 'the sort of girl that blokes shag, more the sort their mums would like them to marry'. Talk about damning with faint praise! When you are trying your best to be a naughty, wannabe wild child, the last thing you want to hear is that you'd make someone a nice little wife! The worst of it was, Wendy secretly thought so too. She found the whole messy business of anonymous fumbling around on top of the coats in the bedroom; standing around in your bare feet on unknown kitchen floors sticky with Lord knows what; and forever listening to your new best friend pour out her heart about what a bastard, Tim or Kevin or Barry was, all rather unpleasant. Halfway through her final year, Wendy decided that she had had quite enough of drugs and casual sex; that is to say, two joints, both of which made her vomit copiously, and two boyfriends, one in her first year who she went out with for six months and didn't sleep with and another in her second year with whom she had uncomfortable, although not unpleasant, sex on three occasions in a Datsun Cherry in a four-week period and who had then dumped her to go back to his former girlfriend who he hadn't officially broken up with anyway.

She applied for teacher-training college and a year and a half later got a job teaching art at an Oxford comprehensive school. Life went on with just a few more downs than ups, as is often the case for young teachers, and Wendy moved schools and painted in her spare time. By her later twenties the ups and downs had called a truce and Wendy, while not exactly happy was content, although she felt she was becoming decidedly spinsterish at an early age. But it wasn't her age, it was her attitude. She had no interest in casual relationships, although there had been a couple of minor flings. She wanted – she didn't know what – not great passion but a good, kind man who loved her and who would show her the affection she had been denied by her mother after her father had left. So far, there had been no likely candidates. She didn't mind too much. Just occasionally when her mother called to find out how she was, in other words, to find out whether she had met a man yet, gleefully waiting for a negative answer which would enable her to launch into another flinty-voiced lecture, Wendy would have liked, just once, to have been able to confound her by saying she had met the most wonderful man in the world. Still, she didn't complain at her lot. She was now an established, and very good, art teacher in a small school in Hampshire and had even sold a fair few of her paintings via a local restaurant. She gave extra lessons to the owner's daughter, who was very talented and in return, her father let Wendy put her paintings on the walls of the restaurant with a discreet price tag attached. The owner took a modest commission which paid for the extra art lessons for his daughter, so everyone was happy.

Then one blustery, grisly afternoon, Wendy bumped into Fraser. Literally. It was in the Tesco's car park in Aldershot. Wendy was distracted, thinking about her latest painting which was refusing to cooperate and Fraser was in a hurry, dashing to pick up a few luxuries like chocolate, vitamins and decent shower gel which he would need in the coming months in Afghanistan. They sedately reversed into each other and as soon as each emerged from their respective car to apologise rather than remonstrate, they fell totally in love. Fraser was a sergeant in the parachute regiment getting ready to go off to fight in Helmand. He was due to leave in ten days and this was one of his final opportunities to do a bit of last-minute essential shopping. They chatted for an hour and a half in the car park and Fraser took Wendy to dinner the following evening. From that moment, they spent every spare, precious second they could together. The weekend before Fraser was due to leave, he managed to call in a few favours and get a pass out for 48 hours. They went to the New Forest and spent two days not seeing much beyond the bedroom of the little guesthouse. On the Sunday evening as they sat together in his car in front of the house where Wendy lived on the ground floor, the top story belonging to an often absent AA man, Fraser asked Wendy to marry him. She cried, laughed, kissed him and told him to come back safely from his tour of duty. Fraser looked crestfallen.

"What's the matter?" laughed Wendy through her tears.

"You didn't actually answer the question," said Fraser mournfully.

Flinging her arms around his neck and covering his eyes, cheeks and lips with a thousand kisses, Wendy cried, "Each kiss is a thousand times *yes, yes, yes!*"

She stood on the pavement long after he had driven off gazing in the direction his car had gone and only went in when the chill of the evening finally found its way through the warmth of her glow. It was the last time she ever saw him. The shock of Fraser's death in a friendly-fire incident two months later brought on the miscarriage.

She gave in her notice, went out to spend a few months with her father, who had just taken early retirement and had bought his dream villa in Portugal, paid the briefest of visits to her mother who told her to get over it and find herself another man, preferably one not engaged in a hazardous profession, and finally got a job as assistant head of the art department in a decent secondary school in Essex. She stayed there gathering dust, extra pounds on her waistline and a semi-regular series of weekend hangovers for a dozen years. She occasionally endeavoured to pull herself together; the spontaneous gym membership had been the result of one such attempt, but she gradually found herself sliding into middle age unloved and unloving. She never painted now and concentrated on encouraging the potential of her better students and nursing the less able ones to acquit themselves well enough for exams. Birthdays, Christmases and long summer holidays came and went and Wendy barely noticed their passing.

When her father died and left her the villa, she had thought of moving out there with her savings which amounted to quite a tidy sum as she hadn't taken a foreign holiday in years and spent little money on herself save her packet of Silk Cut every other day, a decent bottle of wine or three at weekends, and as much ice-cream as she wanted. However, she decided against the move for no clear reason other than the seemingly oldest law of physics that inertia is the strongest of all forces.

Yet, a couple of years later, Wendy received a call from her former student whose father had the restaurant in Hampshire and suddenly felt very old as this young girl, as she remembered her, was now herself an art teacher in Devizes in Wiltshire. It was her first year out of college and she had spent a year teaching and saving up before intending to head off backpacking around the world in search of artistic inspiration and cheap hallucinogens. She was calling to tell Wendy that the head of the art department at her school was retiring and, if Wendy was interested, she would put in a good word with the headteacher as he was a golf buddy of her father's. Three months later, Wendy took up temporary residence with the antisocial geography teacher and put in an offer on an old farm cottage in a village some four miles outside Devizes.

She had planned to do up the cottage and spend her time reading and painting again and to slide gracefully towards the age where it didn't really matter anymore whether she shaved her legs every other day and where no one noticed if she wore the same outfit three days a week. The final proof would be when the other female teachers, and the wives of the male ones, were always nice to her since they no longer perceived her as a sexual predator or threat, a phenomenon which most art teachers appear, at some time or another, to have been suspected of.

And so, there she sat, nursing a cooling cup of coffee and a dull throb in her temples in her charming kitchen surrounded by packing crates and cardboard boxes feeling fat; closing in on fifty at an alarming rate and yet, surprisingly serene now that she had made up her mind to accept her fate. She had her eyes closed, partly against the pain in her inflamed brain and partly because she was trying to work out in her mind's eye the detail for a painting she was working on, when there was a loud metallic clang as the hinge on the letter-box snapped shut. Simultaneously, Wendy started and winced as she felt the clang resonate around her skull amplified by a factor of ten and rising as steadily as she could from her chair, she wandered into the hall and up to the pile of post on the doormat. It wasn't much of a pile, just a leaflet from the local supermarket boasting that its doors would be open until 10pm on Christmas Eve (Wendy felt sorry for the check-out girls, forced to stay at work like so many Bob Cratchits), an envelope containing a 'Happy Holidays and Best Wishes' card from the school's board of governors (no signature) and a small, very worn and dirty ivory coloured postcard decorated with what seemed like a sprig of holly and some faded blue and red silk-like material on it.

Puzzled, Wendy turned the card over and saw it was addressed to the cottage but to a Miss Amy Hobbs. The day and month of the date were smudged but there was no doubt over the year, 1916. Taking the card carefully between her hands as she would have handled a hot casserole dish, Wendy carried it over to the kitchen window and read it. Then she read it again and again until the words blurred before her eyes and she had to be careful not to add her tears to the single drop shed by the Scottish nurse onto the ink ninety years before. She suddenly thought of Fraser, killed in a faraway land two days after his last email. Of course, she didn't know what had become of this Walter or his dearest Amy but she suddenly felt moved to find out. She felt that receiving this card, just at that moment in her life, was almost a sign of something. Wendy didn't believe in fate or destiny or God or anything more spiritual than a few vague notions that inspiration came in the unlikeliest of forms and from the most bizarre sources sometimes. But she knew she was in Amy's cottage and that Amy had had a sweetheart who was away in a war and who had loved her and thought of her. For Wendy, that was inspiration enough to discover more. It would have to wait until after Christmas, she reasoned. Then she would go to see the vicar and introduce herself (although she admitted that she would be a very inactive parishioner. She couldn't actually remember the last occasion she had been inside a church) and see if he could help her look at the parish records. In the meantime, she felt sure she could find the regiment from the blue and red ribbon on the postcard with a little help from Mr Google. Her hangover now disappeared, Wendy set the postcard down on her easel which was about the only furniture she had unpacked apart from the bottle opener, a single wine glass, two coffee mugs, one of which was currently serving as her makeshift ashtray and a few odd plates and saucers, and went and took a long hot shower. Padding back into the kitchen, now wrapped in a ridiculously fluffy white dressing gown (nicked from the Grand Suite cabin on the *QEII* by her dear old dad), Wendy cleared the table and wiped it down and taking the postcard, a sketch pad and a charcoal crayon from their temporary resting place on the easel, made a few brief sketches of the card both front and back and found herself actually looking forward to Christmas for the first time in years.

★★★

Over three thousand miles away, in Toronto, Amy's great grandson, Keith, was having difficulty sleeping. He often did the night before taking a flight. Keith loved airports and planes and as a child had dreamed of becoming a commercial jet pilot. Asthma had put pay to that idea and instead he helped others to fly in big planes and became a travel agent. At the age of 49, he now had his own agency catering to independent travellers and he loved his job. His mother, Amy's granddaughter, Denise, had come to Canada on a plane on one of the very first commercial passenger flights between London and Montreal when she was 4 years old after the Second World War with her mum, Elsie, (the daughter of Amy and Walter) and her Canadian flying-officer father, Joe, who took them away from rationing and worn out little England to a new life in Calgary and a farm bigger than a small English county, as Elsie always said. That was the only occasion his mother had ever been in a plane and she never forgot it and Keith supposed his love of planes and travel came from there. When Keith's grandparents retired in the sixties, they sold the farm and moved out to Vancouver while Denise and her husband, Keith Sr. and little son moved east to Toronto to start up in the dry-cleaning business. They had a small chain of six shops and did well, and when, in turn, they sold up and retired to Florida, Keith Jr. had already had his own travel agency for nearly ten years. He had married too young and divorced but remained on good terms with his ex-wife, Carol, and saw his twin girls, Alice and Amy, very often. The girls were now both at Toronto's York University; Alice studying law, and Amy, English Literature.

This Christmas, Keith was to have the holiday he had dreamed of for many years. He was going to trace the English side of his family. His father's side had originally come from Italy and Keith had immensely enjoyed his visit to a small village near Naples with the girls three or four years previously, where they met several people with a similar surname who all immediately claimed to be long-lost relations and spoiled their three Canadian cousins rotten. What he did know was that his mother, Denise, had been born in Norfolk in the east of England because that's where her father had been stationed and Elsie, her mum, was a WAAF at the same base. Elsie knew that she had been born in 1917 in Wiltshire on a farm but couldn't say more than that because the flu epidemic of 1919 had carried off her mother, Amy and Amy's parents. All she remembered was being taken on a train by a woman who smelled of cough mixture and what she later discovered to be gin, to an orphanage. The woman, Miss Brown, who Elsie later assumed to have been some sort of proto-social worker since she never revealed her first name or how she was connected to Elsie, had visited her several times over the next few years and told her that her mother's name was Amy Hobbs and that she was born in a village in Wiltshire. Miss Brown told her neither the name of the village nor the name of her father, and Elsie was too young to think much more about it. The orphanage was no luxury hotel but it wasn't a Dickensian workhouse either and Elsie learned to read and write, and was polite and sweet-natured, and at the age of fourteen was taken on as a second lady's maid by a well-meaning Bloomsbury type and went to live in Hampstead. When the war broke out, Elsie, thanks to the progressiveness of her employer, was encouraged to join up and, due to an instinctive gift for arithmetic and the calmest of temperaments under pressure, was assigned to the be a flight plotter on an bomber airbase in Norfolk, which is where she met Joe.

It wasn't much to go on, but Keith Jr. had done some research on the internet and had discovered two or three villages in Wiltshire where there had been several families named Hobbs. His plan was to visit these villages to see whether he could discover the record of Elsie's birth in the parish registers and to spend some time in the land of his fathers, or more accurately, mothers. He already had a list of the vicars of the three villages he thought were most likely and felt that making contact with them to arrange a visit immediately after Christmas would be the best place to start.

As for what happened next? Well, everybody likes a happy ending.

THE AUTHOR

My name is Nancy Drew. Really! And yes, if I had a nickel, or even a penny for every comment, wisecrack and raised eyebrow that my name has invoked over the last thirty-odd years, I would be very, very rich. Well, actually I am pretty comfortably off, but not because of my name and the little injection of wealth is recent and a surprise. I certainly wasn't expecting it.

I only started one day because the TV was on the fritz and I couldn't watch my soaps.

And I wasn't born Nancy Drew. I was born Nancy Wisniewski, right here in Ottawa. The Drew came attached to my husband, Jeffrey, when we got married in the Fall of 1981. That's him now, banging about in the basement. It's Sunday afternoon and Jeff is building a cocktail bar for the basement den. I ask you, a cocktail bar! He doesn't even drink cocktails! But he and the guys have this competition as to who has the best basement. Larry, originally from Aberdeen and Jeff's co-worker from the Rogers office, has an Olhausen Excalibur pool table in his; Habib, our neighbourhood veterinarian, who was born in Beirut, has a 65-inch flat-screen Samsung LED TV in his; and our next-door neighbour, Ian, originally from Buffalo, has installed several vintage arcade games including a 1976 Captain Fantastic Elton

John pinball machine (when Ian had it delivered, his partner, also a musician in the Ottawa Symphony Orchestra, William, rolled his eyes and said, "Honey, I think everyone already knows we're gay. Do we *have* to gild the lily quite so much?"). So, you see, Jeff just had to build the cocktail bar.

Honestly, I don't know why they bother. All they end up doing if the Senators aren't on TV is play Texas hold'em and talk about snow tires, from what I can tell! But boys will be boys, even if the youngest of these particular boys won't see fifty again!

But I don't mind. When it's our turn to host, I make up some sandwiches and make sure Jeff has remembered to buy in plenty of Rickard's Red and OJ for Ian who has been on the wagon for fifteen years ever since he nearly lost a hand when he took out a tree in his Nissan and, "Losing a hand for a professional violinist is never a good idea," as Ian said when he got out of hospital. Then I go and pick up Sonya, Habib's wife who was also born in Lebanon but to a Druze father and a Quebecker journalist mother and we go to the movies or try out a new restaurant (last week it was Gezellig in Westboro, delicious! Try the Beef Daube, it's to die for!). Sometimes we meet up with Rachel, Larry's ex-wife who is a nurse at the Ottawa Hospital. Larry knows we are still friends with Rachel but we don't rub it in. So the boys have their evenings and get to win or lose a few Loonies and argue about sports or the government or which actress is the hottest (William may be gay, but according to Jeff, he has a real soft spot for Liv Tyler) and we get our girls' night and talk about... what do we talk about? The news? Never! Politics? Not likely! Same goes for sports, although Sonya is a secret Habs fan but she keeps that quiet in Ontario! And we certainly don't talk about our men! We talk, like most middle-aged mothers who (apart from Rachel) have always been homemakers, about three things: our children and grandchildren; when and where we are going to retire; and, tragic to say, what we are currently watching on TV or have just read in a glossy magazine.

Pretty standard stuff, really. And along with these everyday lives comes the usual catalogue of joys and woes. For us, they are things like our daughter Caroline's graduation from Toronto despite her dyslexia, and her wedding to Daniel three years ago but subsequently learning she can't have kids and the angst of deciding whether to face the process of adopting. Or our son Paul being made Lieutenant Commander in the navy and taking command of a Kingston-class coastal defence vessel out of Halifax, and finally marrying Sarah two years ago, after ten years living together and having two beautiful boys, Aaron and Bradley, and losing one, Ben, to sudden infant death syndrome, or Jeff's prostate cancer scare (thankfully caught early and cured). Just the usual. For Rachel and Larry, the pain of an acrimonious divorce after twenty-three years of marriage, or their son, Damien, getting married at eighteen to Julie when they were both still in high school and six months later, Julie presenting them with grandchildren; triplets, all girls! Ten years on and Damien has his own cab firm now and Julie works the dispatch from home. And at least the grandchildren have ensured that Larry and Rachel are civil with each other these days. For Sonya and Habib their woes were so many and so harrowing during the strife in Lebanon that they seldom mention them, but since coming to Canada in the late eighties, they too have settled into the gentle and sometimes not so gentle ups and downs of suburban life. Their son, Ali, has just graduated med school but wants to go and work in the Democratic Republic of Congo with Medecin Sans Frontieres! His parents are proud and mortified all at the same time. As for Ian and William, we never talk about it now, – they were so afraid of telling us, so sure we would shun them, but we all got past that – but if they can live with William's HIV (ironically, contracted before the screening of blood in 1985 became mandatory, during a transfusion after a simple slip on the ice took him through a glass door outside the Mall), so can we. William says he is blessed which may seem an odd way to look at his affliction. Yet since only 4% of people diagnosed with HIV thirty years ago are still alive today, I can understand his sentiment. William has nearly died a dozen times but with the steadfast love and support from Ian, an amazing will to live and latterly, with the help of ARVs, he is still making us laugh with his waspish wit, and cry with the beauty of his skill on the cello.

As I said, pretty standard stuff really. Until a couple

of years ago, that is, when, one Tuesday afternoon in February, the TV suddenly had a meltdown just before *The Young and the Restless*.

A long time ago, back before I was Nancy Drew, during that wet, chaotic, glorious summer of '76 when Montreal hosted the world at the Olympic Games, my dad, Lazlo Wisniewski got me a summer job at the perfume counter at the Bay. Dad worked as a tailor in the gentleman's outfitters department when even the off-the-peg suits were individually finished. An apprentice tailor in the family business in Katowice before the war, he learned to fly in a Polish-built RWD5 monoplane. He was taught to fly by a baron no less, for whose family his family had been making suits for generations and who noticed young Lazlo's eyes light up every time he spoke of flying. So the Baron, who was eccentric but a generous soul, taught him, much to my grandmother's horror. The Baron Karol, who had been one of the first Poles ever to fly a plane, and, despite his advanced age and lofty rank, insisted on joining a squadron just before the Germans invaded. My dad, who was not quite seventeen at the time, followed him and, with the Baron's help, lied about his age and found himself in the open cockpit of a PZL P.11 on the 1st September 1939. Neither he nor the Baron got off the ground. The airstrip was bombed by a group of Stukas and the Baron's plane took a direct hit, while Dad was thrown clear of his aircraft by the force of a nearby explosion. In his raw inexperience, he hadn't even fastened his seatbelt and that is what saved his life. Along with a few survivors, he originally tried to make his way to join up with what little was left of the army but decided that rather than commit noble suicide, he wanted to live and fight the Nazis. It took him weeks of hiding in barns, moving only at night and eventually, with the help of a courageous Estonian fisherman, he made it to England. He spoke no English and all he had with him was his Polish Air Force identity card. Within eight weeks he was back flying again. He flew a Hurricane in the Battle of Britain in the 303 Polish Fighter Squadron.

In late 1944, invalided out after taking almost a year to recover from a very bad crash-landing in which he broke both legs and sustained severe burning to about a third of his body, he left for Canada with his new young English bride, my mum, Betty, who had been a cook at the hospital where dad was laid up for the first four months after the crash. They settled in Hamilton at first but after my brothers Jake and Mateusz were born in 1949 and 1952, they moved to Ottawa. Dad got a job at the Bay, Mum became a school dinner lady at the newly opened Viscount Alexander public school and by the time I was born in 1958 as something of a surprise (my mum, bless her heart, always called me a surprise rather than an accident), we lived in the top half of a townhouse in the poorer end of Sandy Hill.

Mum and Dad have been married for seventy years this year (Dad is 92, Mum is 86) and are living in a retirement community in Amelia in northern Florida with an on-site nurse in the 'village'. We fly down for Canadian Thanksgiving as it is in October and the tickets are cheaper. And the whole family is making the trip this year to celebrate their – what is a seventieth anniversary called? Hang on, I will look it up... Well I never knew that! According to Google, their platinum anniversary. Jake and Mateusz will be there. Actually, Jake is thinking of moving to Amelia himself next year from Calgary when he retires. Annie, his wife, died three years ago from pancreatic cancer and his kids, Jeannie and Samantha, are living in the States in Colorado and Oregon with families of their own, so they will be there too, I hope. Mateusz went to Poland after the whole Lech Walesa, Solidarnosc movement to teach English and he is still there, living in Krakow, where he owns a car hire franchise and is married to Olga. They have four kids of their own, 2 boys and 2 girls and– I can never remember – eight or nine grandchildren. I need to check the emails. It might be more! When Jeff and I went out there five years ago to see them, I think they already had seven and Ela was seven months pregnant with Janusz and I am sure there have been at least a couple of additions since then! Mateusz is selling up this year and he wants to bring the whole clan to Amelia for the party. He probably will too. They are going to have to charter their own plane at this rate!

★★★

Sorry about that, that was Jeff. Hammer made contact with thumb and the air was a trifle blue for a moment! He's gone out to Canadian Tire for some more nails. He left in a huff because I suggested he swing by Drug Mart on his way back for some Band-Aids!

Oh, I didn't tell you how Jeffrey and I met! Well, I left school in May of 1977, three days before my birthday and went to work full time at the Bay, only this time in ladies fashion. A year or so, no, it was almost exactly two years after I started, we were still living in Sandy Hill but the boys were working out in Alberta on building sites, Dad was now head of gentleman's outfitting (as he called the men's department until the day he retired at 65 in 1987) at Sears and Mum still cooked up huge vats of mince and potatoes at the Alexander. We had lots of room since Dad had managed to buy the downstairs half of the house when old Mr Jennings had to go into a nursing home. Oh, I lost my thread then... just a second... oh yes! So there I am hanging up the latest seamless support bras from Playtex when I hear an embarrassed cough behind me. No matter how long you worked in 'women's', it was always a hoot to see how embarrassed the guys got when they came in to buy something racy for their sweethearts. These days, embarrassment is a thing of the past what with the internet and main street stores like, Aren't We Naughty? Anyway, I turned round and there was this tall, blond, blue-eyed kid, maybe a couple of years older than me, with bright crimson cheeks and stammering incoherently. It turned out he was to be the best man at his big brother's wedding later that month and he had been given the task by his pals at Bell Canada of buying something sexy to put on the blow-up doll that someone had got hold of by mail order for the stag. He was so cute, huffing and puffing and it took me about twenty minutes to prise the story out of him. Eventually I sorted him out with some see-through red negligee, which no woman in her right mind would have ever bought unless she was working in, what the law called, a 'bawdy house'! Then I did something very daring. Just as this cute guy was thanking me for the hundredth time and taking up his purchase, which I had carefully wrapped in plain white paper before slipping it into a Hudson's Bay carrier bag, and this time it was my turn to blush, I suddenly blurted out, "Hey, would you like to have coffee with me some time?"

And bless him, without a moment's hesitation or awkwardness, he said, "Sure! That'd be cool! Er... I'm Jeffrey, Jeff." And he rather sweetly and rather formally extended his hand.

Taking it with a slight curtsey I said, "Hi Jeffrey Jeff, I'm Nancy."

Two days after that we went and had a coffee at Tim Horton's and one year and three very brief and very silly break ups and reconciliations later, we got engaged. We got married a year after that and Jeff returned the favour and asked his brother Lionel to be his best man. I sent

Lionel a black see-through negligee through the post with a note saying, 'Just in case this one prefers black!' A year after we were married, Paul was born and I quit my job at the Bay to take up my new role as full-time mum. Poor Lionel, he died a few years later from a massive heart attack. We don't see his widow, Sadie anymore and there were no children.

Oh, now I am all out of order! It must be my age! I meant to tell you about my 'writing career' before meltdown Tuesday!

Where was I? Oh yes, so dear old Dad got me a temp job at the Bay. I will never forget it. I was not long turned eighteen and it was the day when young Michel Vaillancourt won the silver medal in the show jumping in his hometown. We were all gathered round one of the television sets that had been set up throughout the store for the Olympics and I remember us all yelling and screaming at the screen, willing Michel on. As I was going back to my station, my friend Yvonne, who worked in ladies' accessories, asked me if I was going to enter the competition.

"What competition?"

"Oh, Nancy, don't you ever read the notice board in the staff canteen?" she asked me exasperatedly.

"Not today I haven't… what competition?"

"Here!" and Yvonne handed me a flyer with the Hudson Bay logo at the top which said that the management were running a competition as part of the new marketing campaign and were offering $250 in store vouchers to any member of staff who could come up with a slogan for the launch of the autumn range.

I shrugged, "Why would that be of interest to me?"

"Because it's $250 and you are always thinking up clever things to say!"

"Am I? Or are you just telling me in your own sweet way that I am a smart mouth?" I laughed. It was true, I had a bit of a reputation for making wisecracks at school. Poor Miss Weatherspoon, my geography teacher. I still blush when I remember calling her a Miss Jean Brodie who never had a prime!

I took the flyer home and after a couple of hours and with a dozen crumpled sheets of paper strewn around my feet, I purposefully dotted the full stop of my first piece of creative writing that wasn't homework.

I didn't win.

A manager in the publicity department had a quiet word with Dad who had a quiet word with me.

"Listen, Kochanie," he always called me that: it's Polish; the nearest translation would be 'darling', "they didn't want to make a fuss [*how typically Canadian*, I thought] but they just felt that your slogan was a bit inappropriate. After all, it's only been a few years since that Quebec thing, OK? Nobody is mad with you. Just you are young," and with that the matter was closed. And that, until that fateful afternoon two years ago, was the extent of my career as a writer.

What was my slogan?

In large cartoon letters with firework bursts drawn in the background, I had written:

'Come and have a blast at the Bay!'

I was disappointed, mildly, but I gave it no more thought until many years later when Paul was on an immersion course in French because he had a six-month posting coming up as a liaison officer at HMCS *Donnacona*, the naval reserve base in Montreal. I will never understand how just because the navy use a place as a base, they call it a ship even when it's a large building on dry land! Anyway, Paul was staying with us for a couple of weeks; this was just a few months after he met Sarah who was studying at Carleton University in Ottawa. They met while skating on the Rideau Canal, you know. Paul literally swept her off her feet. He later admitted he knocked her down deliberately so he could have a chance to speak to her! Anyway, Paul was wandering around the house all day with a navy issued Sony Walkman with some government French course on tape. Being the supportive mum I am, I invited Sonya over to help him practice. Sonya's mother came from Quebec City and Sonya spoke French, English and Arabic fluently. Well, Paul was grateful for the help and I was enthralled listening to him and Sonya jabber away... my handsome son, so clever and in French too! I caught a few words and one afternoon, they were doing some sort of role play about shopping. Women can understand shopping in any language, can't we, girls? That suddenly brought back my memories of the Bay and the slogan

47

competition so I told the story and when I explained the slogan, Paul and Sonya looked at each other and burst out laughing. I was a bit vexed at being the butt of the joke but tried not to show it.

"So what was so bad about it?" I asked a tad peevishly.

"Well, Cherie," said Sonya, still mocking me but being very sweet about it, "it may have been borderline in English but the French version would have been something like, 'On va s'eclater chez la Baie!' for the stores in Quebec!"

I was still puzzled and still a little miffed. Paul came over to me and put an arm round me and bent his neck to give me a peck on the cheek.

"Mum," he said as gently as he could but I could hear the laughter bubbling up in his voice, "Mum, "on va s'eclater chez la Baie" can have a literal meaning too." And then the penny dropped. After twenty-eight years, the penny finally dropped. I felt such a fool!

Of course like most Canadians, I knew about the FLQ, the extreme Quebec-based separatist group that carried out a string of attacks including almost a hundred bombings over several years in the late sixties, culminating in 1970 with the kidnapping and murder of Pierre Laporte, who was a minister in the Quebec provincial government, and the October Crisis. I was only about eleven or twelve at the time but I remember seeing Pierre Trudeau on TV just before he invoked the War Measures Act, and watching the news like it was a movie as tanks and soldiers went out onto the streets of Montreal.

I didn't need Paul to say any more. I guessed. When they were gone, I did Google it and, now that I look back on it, a phrase like, 'We're gonna explode at The Bay" does indeed, seem a little inappropriate given the circumstances in that era!

No, I was not writer: I was a watcher. I am a little ashamed to admit it but with two grown-up children, a husband who works office hours and no interest in the gym or pottery classes, I spend my afternoons, once the housework is done and before I make a start on the dinner, watching soaps. I am addicted to the vacuous, often poorly acted and always overacted, continuing serials with their ludicrous plots, cardboard sets, ridiculous dialogue and the cheesy music which punctuates every glance, close-up and dramatic conclusion. They are my friends and I invite them into my living room every weekday from 2pm till 4.30pm. And like all good friends, I overlook their faults and foibles. Woe betide the telemarketer who dares to call during those hours! Not even Caroline or Rachel call me then. Sonya sometimes does but that is only so we can compare notes on what a bitch Brooke is or whether we think Steve will ever find out that the real father of his baby is his brother, Duncan. In my defence, all I can say is that I don't drink in the daytime, I don't do drugs and I don't have a lover. I don't even like chocolate much. My habit, my vice are the soaps; those ridiculous, implausible serials that seduce the viewer into addiction. It's true, you try it. I remember even Habib, who is constantly but good-naturedly teasing Sonya for her soap compulsion, once, a few years ago, put his back out playing golf and was laid up in bed at home for two weeks. By the end of that fortnight he was calling me to express his disbelief that Troy would ever marry that slut, Maria, when everyone knew she had poisoned Brady to get her hands on the insurance money!

Oh my! Is that the time? I better put the potatoes on. Jeff is back – I can hear him stomping about down there. Bear with me, I just get a little carried away sometimes. I'll tell you all about it after dinner when Jeff is watching *Hockey Night*.

★★★

Me again. Jeff is swearing at the screen arguing with Don Cherry, but then again, who doesn't? Jeffrey is third-generation Irish and was born in Bathurst, New Brunswick. But after a row with his alcoholic father when he was sixteen and a perfunctory goodbye to his despised stepmother, Jeff took the eighteen-hundred dollars that he had saved up from working as a clerk in a local grocery store at five bucks a day since he was fourteen when he left school and hobo'd on freight trains to Bangor, Maine in the US. His brother, Lionel, had done more or less the same thing three years earlier and being a little older, at eighteen, had enlisted in the army. Jeff worked in an electrical repair shop and enrolled in night school to learn about the rapidly growing telecommunications technology. After a few years, and having lost his resentment towards his father (who died two years after he left), Jeff took the train back north and in 1974, when he was not quite twenty, he got as job as an engineer's mate, a sort of *un*glorified apprenticeship, with Bell Canada in Ottawa. He stayed with his brother Lionel who had left the army after five years and was living in the mostly French suburb of Vanier working as a mechanic. After Caroline was born in 1984, Jeff who was now head of the emergency repair division was offered a management job at Cantel, the first wireless phone company in Canada just a few months before the service went live. Through various name changes and buy outs over the last thirty years, Jeff has stayed with what is now Rogers Wireless and is now one of the VPs in the technology department, which is ironic considering he always forgets to take his darn cell phone with him whenever he leaves the house! Still, at least we have really fast broadband!

In case any of you are observant and good at math (and Lord knows, I'm not), you may have worked out that I left school just before my birthday in 1977, when I was just about nineteen years old. Yes, I missed a year of school. I forgot to mention it. Well, it was a long time ago. I was 8 and mum was bringing me back from ballet lessons (her idea, not mine) at Madame Lenska's Academy of Dance, which was actually a large open room above a butcher's with a somewhat clumsily installed rail and a mirror. Madame Lenska herself, despite her name, was neither Polish nor Russian; she was a nasal blonde from Brooklyn who, as a young woman, had danced burlesque while she auditioned, without success, for the American Ballet Theatre. So, mum and I caught the bus. I remember it was freezing cold and we had had early snow. It was October and the leaves had all died that year before we got the chance to see them in their full amber, russet and maroon glory. Later on, they told me it was no one's fault, the bus driver swerved to avoid a stray dog and the wheel hit the kerb and the bus flipped over on its side and skidded along causing sparks and screams for nearly a hundred yards. By some miracle the dog ran off unharmed and no one in the bus suffered more than a few cuts and bruises, and the driver got a broken arm. Mum emerged without a scratch. By sheer bloody bad luck, the window next to where I was sitting shattered into a million pieces and amazingly missed me completely, save for one sliver. That darned sliver went straight into my right eye. Apparently, I had whacked my head pretty hard on the back of the seat in front and was out cold, so I didn't feel a thing. When I came to, a couple of days later, in a room with two beds but just mine was occupied (they had sedated me while they operated), I awoke with a thumping headache, three missing front teeth and a broken ankle. I couldn't see anything and I put my hands to my face and felt the thick bandages. That made me panic but I could smell my mum's perfume, she always wore 'Evening in Paris', and I could hear my dad clearing his throat. Mum and Dad were sitting on the edge of the bed and the boys were, so they told me later, standing tearfully behind them. I smiled groggily and said, "Mum, Dad! Where am I? The bus tipped over! Are you ok?"

Dad just squeezed my hand and kissed the top of my head and I heard him stand up and he must have silently guided the boys out of the room.

"Yes, Darling, I'm fine. You gave us all a scare but you are going to be ok, my angel."

"Why can't I see, Mum? I'm scared!"

"It's OK, Nancy, sweetheart, you got a little bit of glass in one of your eyes." I could hear the tremor in her voice as she struggled to fight back the tears.

"Don't cry, Mum. I am sure I will be better soon."

Mum just dissolved into sobs at that point, which made me cry too but with the bandages over my eyes, it was impossible and I just sniffled. Dad must have heard her and come in because I felt the weight of the mattress shift as he sat down beside her. And they stayed there with me, not speaking just stroking my hand, or my hair for what seemed like an eternity. I drifted off to sleep and didn't dream.

I mentioned somewhere that I am a bit of a wiseacre. Well, a week or so later they finally removed the bandages and were fussing around me telling me to keep my eyes closed until they were ready. I could hear my parents and my brothers hovering by my side and they all seemed in much better spirits than the first time that I had been aware that they were all in the room. My little room now had another occupant too. A little girl about my age, who I later learned was called Agatha and who had fallen down some stairs. But she didn't have any visitors and was asleep all the time. I often wonder what happened to her.

I was half ready. The doctor had been talking to me every day and preparing me for what I was about to see. He explained that the tiny shard of glass had gone quite deeply into my right eye and that although they tried, there was nothing they could do and that I would never see out of it again. "But look on the bright side, Nancy," he said, "Your left eye is perfect and now you will be able to wear a patch and look like a real pirate!" I am sure that is exactly what every eight-year-old girl dreamed of in 1966!

So when they finally removed my bandages and fiddled around for a few more moments and held the mirror up to my face, my parents, my brothers and the hospital staff all leaned forward with encouraging smiles. I blinked a few times and winced as the bright light stung my one good eye but after a few seconds, I looked up into the little round mirror that the doctor was holding in front of my face. Looking back at me was a pale, brown-haired girl with a few bruises on her face and a plaster over her left brow and one rather pretty, so I have often been told, hazel eye. Over the right eye was a black patch straight out of *Treasure Island* (the Disney film that was a favourite of my both my brothers). No one spoke while they nervously awaited my reaction.

After a good twenty seconds gazing into the little

mirror I looked around the room at each of them in turn and with a gap-toothed smile, I gave my verdict.

In my best Robert Newton voice, I said, "Yo ho ho and a bottle of rum!"

To this day, when my brothers call me, they start the conversation with, "Arghhh, Jim Lad!"

My collection of patches in different materials and some with diamante studs is quite impressive these days.

So later, back in Miss Abernathy's class again, after the best part of a school year away and being the oldest in my class by at least six months, the other girls called me Cyclops. And have you noticed, little girls can be so cruel? The boys thought I was way cool (which is an expression that was first coined in Canada, I am told. Like so many other great "American" words, it really came from above the 49th parallel; other great words such as 'William' and 'Shatner', 'Keanu' and 'Reeves', and 'Mike' and 'Myers'. OK, we won't mention the words 'Pamela' and 'Anderson'; nobody's perfect!). But I didn't care what anyone said though because I had a sharp wit and two older brothers!

Since then, of course, I have become fascinated with famous one-eyed people and it always gave me an extensive choice for fancy-dress parties growing up. At various times, I have been Colombo (borrowing Jeff's filthy old Mac with an unlit stogie clamped in my teeth), Rex Harrison dressed in tweeds like he was in *My Fair Lady* and Leo McKern as *Rumpole of the Bailey* dressed in a white wig and a black robe. Not too many famous one-eyed women, you will notice, well none that are good characters for a fancy-dress do! My favourite one was for my fortieth birthday. Jeff wanted to organise a fancy dress at our house. I decided not to black up as Sammy Davis Jr (poor taste) or Moshe Dayan (too political) so I opted for Cassandra, the prophetess from Greek mythology. It gave me a fabulous excuse to wear layers of multi-coloured scarves and outrageous makeup. Now I know, technically, Cassandra wasn't blind in either eye but a lot of people believe she was. Cassandra's curse was that all her prophesies came true but no one believed her. For Cassandra you can substitute 'Mum' and for no one I mean 'my kids'!

By way of a couple of illustrations:

"Pauly! Don't pull Caroline's pigtails or she will wallop you!"

Two seconds later: "Owwww! Mum! Caro hit me!"

"Caroline! You better take your Parka if you are going out to play, it's freezing out. You'll catch cold!"

"I'll be alright, Mum!"

Later that evening: "Achoo! Mum, can I sday ad home tomorrow, I feel icky!"

Anyway, as I said, most people wrongly think that Cassandra's trade-off for seeing the future was the fact she was blind. Most people. But some folk are better educated in the classics than others and I forgot that Habib was from the Levant! So, everyone starts arriving and we are having a great time when Habib comes up to me and looking me up and down asks, "Nance, who are you supposed to be?"

"Why, Cassandra of course!"

"Well, I thought Cassandra wasn't blind."

"See," I said, "I knew you were going to say that!"

Smart mouth, see what I mean?

Anyway, so there I am, at precisely two o'clock on a really icy February afternoon, two years ago next week, sitting at the breakfast bar in the kitchen. (I don't know why, but I always feel guilty watching TV in the living room on the sofa during the day. At least this way, if someone comes to the door, I can instantly look like I am busy rather than have to struggle out of the couch! My, what a strange old bird I have become!) I have the remote in my hand and I click onto channel 147 for today's fix of the *Young and the Restless* just as the piano music, 'Nadia's Theme' starts and the opening credits, the new ones, begin the damn TV fizzes and dies! I curse but I don't panic, there are two other sets in the house, one in the lounge and one in the basement. Jeff and I won't have one in the bedroom. We read and hey, we may be pushing 60 but we can still occasionally find something more fun to do than fall asleep in front of the TV of a night. Oh my! I hope Caroline doesn't read this! She will be so embarrassed. I can just picture her now; fingers stuck in her ears, eyes tight shut singing, "La-la-la," at the top of her voice! She still does it at 30 years old, just like when she was a little girl.

So, I ran into the lounge with the kitchen remote still in my hand and tried to turn on the TV. Silly cow! I berated myself using my mum's favourite expression for her late sister, Glenda, back in Sussex. I threw down the kitchen remote and rummaged around for the lounge remote. After a mad scramble diving deep into the cushions, I surfaced, red-faced and still cursing with the remote, and pointed and zapped. Nothing happened. "This cannot be happening," I shouted out loud at the black screen. The bloody batteries had gone. How many times have I told Jeff they were about to die?

"Sure, Hon, I'll take care of it." At this point, I was ready to take care of him had he been around!

OK, so the remote doesn't work, surely there must be some buttons or knobs on the set. Well, so you would think. But frisking the entire surface back, front, top and bottom of the flat screen, all I could find was one lousy button. So I hit it and the little red light at the base of the set disappeared. So, I hit it again, and the little red light came back on… but nothing else. Now furious and frantic and yet, slightly ashamed of myself for getting so worked up over a soap opera, I ran downstairs to the basement only to find the television covered in a dustsheet because Jeff was painting the walls. Ripping the dustsheet off the set, I got lucky because the remote was there on top of the TV. I swept it up and steadying my hand, deliberately took aim and 'click', 'click'. OK, third time's a charm 'click'. I think I started to cry. I went to the back of the TV and the lead did not have a plug on it. Jeff must have either been about to replace a fuse or had used the plug for some other device like his power drill or some such. He was always doing that!

The amount of times he takes a good light bulb out of *my* bedside lamp to put in the basement or the garage beggars belief! Three televisions and not a damn one was I able to watch!

I was miffed beyond words and swore up and down I would deal with Jeffrey when he got in from work. That part was all bluster. We seldom argued and certainly not about trivia. Although at that precise moment it was not at all trivial to me, and Jeff was still in the stocks in my mind's eye getting pelted with rotten tomatoes.

I picked up the phone and dialled Sonya. No answer! Then I remembered that she and Habib had taken a couple of days off to go and see Barry Manilow on Broadway.

The outrage over, I was left with a pubescent pout and a huffy shrug and wandered listlessly back to the kitchen and sat down deliberately hard on the stool, somehow punishing it for my woes with my slightly-wider-than-I-would-have-liked bum.

I picked up the TV Guide from the breakfast bar and read the one-line synopsis for *The Young and the Restless*. All it said was, 'Carmine is surprised to see Abby back in town'. No help at all.

I poured myself a cup of coffee from the filter machine and added a Sweet'n Low, then went to the cupboard and got a Reese's Peanut Butter Cup, which defeated the object of the sugar substitute in my coffee but sometimes a girl just has to cope with an emergency as best she can!

I sipped my coffee and nibbled at my sickly treat, staring at the black oblong screen at the end of the breakfast bar, imagining the dialogue and how today's episode would unfold. Then I got to wondering if the actors knew that they were making chewing gum for the brain, and whether the chiselled features and perfect teeth of the men, and the amazing hair and perfect teeth of the women masked anyone of depth or learning, anyone who wasn't as plastic in real life as they seemed on the screen. And that is when, at a few months short of my fifty-fifth birthday, I got it. Inspiration. I hadn't been seeking it, expecting it, nor had any interest in it. But there it was just the same. What if I wrote a book or a story about a soap opera? Not a soap opera itself but a story set behind the scenes about the actors and writers and crew and their real lives (as I imagined them). I knew a lot about the process because seven years ago when Jeff and Habib and Larry went off to catch shad in the Annapolis River in Nova Scotia, Sonya and I flew out to Los Angeles for a week (poor Rachel couldn't make it because she couldn't get the time off work). We spent it doing the Universal Studios tour, the tour of celebrity homes and all the cheesy Hollywood stuff that we loved and that our menfolk just could not understand. It was our secret world, and one into which they frankly didn't want to step! The highlight had been, what is often called, a 'fan event'. It was at the Sheraton at Universal City, and there were cast and crew from several of the soaps that we watched, and they signed autographs, posed for pictures and there were even some question and answer sessions. There were hundreds of middle-aged women there, and surprisingly some younger ones too, and more than a handful of really good-looking guys who I assumed were actors on the few soaps I couldn't fit into my afternoon window. Ian and William laughed when I was excitedly telling them about our trip a couple of weeks later.

"Oh you poor sweet, misguided girl," sighed Ian, cupping my face and shaking his head mournfully.

"What all of them?" I asked.

"Every last queen!" said William.

"Well," I said, "thanks for setting the record straight as it were!"

So, yes I had been watching soaps for thirty-five years, and I had had a taste of Hollywood and had seen some of these creatures up close. I read the gossip magazines not for facts but because it's standard fodder for soap addicts, and although we don't believe 90% of what we read, it is quite entertaining and there is that delicious possibility that ten per cent of it *is* true!

A couple of days later, the lounge TV now having a fully functioning remote with long-life batteries and the kitchen TV to be replaced shortly, I watched my daily quota through completely different eyes. I was no longer a soap fan but a keen observer of clues to the real lives of the characters. I started to write a story. I called it *Behind the Scenes*; a hackneyed cliché, yes, true, but so are the soaps and that is why we love them. The villains are just as identifiable in the *Bold and the Beautiful* as the baddie in *The Lone Ranger* was because of his black hat.

So, I wrote my story about the real-life tragedy and drama of a couple of my favourite stars. Obviously I changed the names of the shows and the characters but anyone like me, anyone who has been watching closely for so many years, would know who they were. It took me three months to write then another three months to write it all over again. I wrote for just an hour or so a day, Monday to Thursday, and a couple of hours on a Sunday, and when it was finished I showed it to Rachel and Sonya and they loved it; mostly because they love me, but the encouragement was nice. They insisted I try to get it published. The thing was, I had no idea what to do with it. Who was I going to send it to? Even Jeff, bless him, pretended to read it and made nice noises and asked around at the PR department at Rogers because he had heard that Katey, one of the senior secretaries there, had a sister down in Austin who was an accountant at Circe Books. I met Katey for coffee one morning and gave her the manuscript. I didn't want to email it because it seemed less real to me. The deal was she would read it and, if she liked it, she would send a copy to her sister and we would all keep our fingers crossed. Katey didn't just like the story, she loved it! I was so elated; I think I twirled in the middle of the Elgin Street!

Well, as it turned out lots of women in publishing, and not just secretaries, watch soaps and like them. It is the secret vice of many of these successful women who have to spend all day in business suits fighting wolves; they can't wait to get home, put on their sweatpants and watch their shows on TiVo with a large glass of Chardonnay and a tub of Ben & Jerry's. Yes, the sisterhood of soap is a broad church!

After another couple of months working with a very sweet and very patient editor, Claire, who gave up so much of her time to help me, my story appeared in a women's new writing magazine called, rather seductively, *Vixen in the November in Eastern Texas*, and I got paid $800 for it. I was truly delighted and then just before Christmas I got a call from a woman called Rebecca who is head of commissioning at Pandora Studios in Chicago. They make TV shows and documentaries mostly aimed at a female market and are very successful. Rebecca wanted to fly me down to the Windy City to discuss a possible project after the holidays. January came around and I flew down with Sonya and Rachel this time, not as glamorous as *Sex in the City* but we were treated like VIPs, and I spent two days locked in a very plush boardroom with Rebecca discussing the possible project.

So here we are; it's a year on from that meeting in Chicago and they are making a three part mini-series from my story! The funny thing is that, they don't want me to write any of the script as they have teams of writers who do that for a living. They are paying me quite a silly amount of money to be a script consultant, whatever that is. I said that as long as Sonya, Rachel and I get to be there when they are making the programmes, they could call me whatever they liked! And frankly, between you and me, I think that I was good for just the one story and I may leave it there, but I know one thing: I had a blast!

★★★

Hello again. I know it has been almost two years since we last spoke but I thought I would bring you up to date. It has been a topsy-turvy couple of years, I must say. We have had some successes, some failures, sadly, three deaths and, happily, two births, so I suppose the balance sheet evens out in a way.

The sad, sad, sad news is that in the last twenty-four months we lost dear William, my old mum, Betty, and poor innocent sweet Ali, Habib and Sonya's only child. He never even made it to Congo. He went to Paris for a year's training in tropical diseases and on his last night of studies, he was on his scooter on the way home and a drunk driver sideswiped him at an intersection. Ali tried to keep his balance but the scooter went over with Ali pinned underneath it with a broken leg. By terrible, tragic bad luck, the petrol tank ignited and he was engulfed in flame. Some passers-by, including an off duty gendarme, tried to save him but the heat was too intense. Poor darling. He burned to death. Sonya was in pieces and came to stay with me and Jeff while Habib went off to Paris to identify the body. To be honest, he could only identify a birthmark on Ali's left shoulder. Once the paperwork was completed, Jeff and I flew out to Paris with Sonya and we buried him there. They have borne it so well and we saw a lot of them in the months that followed but six or seven months ago, they decided they couldn't stay in the house where they had raised Ali; too many sad memories and Habib was close to retirement. So they sold up his veterinary practice and the house, moved down to New Mexico and bought a small ranch that they want to turn into an animal rescue centre. I suppose with Habib being a vet, Sonya being an animal lover and being comfortably off, it makes sense. Actually, I think they both have a deep need to take care, protect and shower affection on living things. Too old to adopt and with no grandchildren, I can see the attraction in caring for abandoned animals. They left a couple of months back with sincere promises to keep in touch. I hope they do, but I would also understand if they don't.

★★★

I can't just give you a litany of death all in one go; it's too clinical and too difficult. So, let me tell you what happened about the mini-series. Now that was an adventure! Remember my story was called, *Behind The Scenes*? Well, that was the first thing they changed! It got called *Behind The Curtain*, which, if you ask me, just emphasises how silly the whole thing is! When they sent me the script for my 'comments' which they wholeheartedly ignored, I showed it to Jeff. He reckoned they should have called it 'Between The Sheets' given all the 'love' scenes they had inserted. Jeff teases me still about being a soft-porn screenwriter and when he insisted on calling Caroline and reading out, complete with character voices, a scene to her, the one where Gary, the daytime heartthrob from *Surgeons* ends up in bed with Felicia *and* her on-screen sister, Diana from *Hearts and Minds*, I could hear Caroline's, "La-la-la," from the receiver from where I was standing on the other side of the kitchen! Karma, however, intervened and Jeff was laughing so hard that he a fit of coughing so violent he strained some muscles in his stomach and had to go to the doctor!

In the end, I never made it to the filming because that was about the time William got sick and to be honest, while I am not a prude, I felt a bit queasy about being on set at what really was quite a saucy show. The funny thing is, it never got released; something to do with distribution rights or syndication problems or something. All I do know is that I got another generous cheque and the show is sitting on a shelf somewhere gathering dust. I hope it stays that way! Jeff was disappointed. He had been looking forward to seeing my name as the inspiration for some televised smut! Mind you, we keep the script by the bed for inspiration, if I can be so crude! Don't tell Caroline! She isn't a prude either but the very suspicion of a hint of a thought of her parents 'doing it' creeps her out so much. Paul teases her about it all the time, "But Caro... how do you think we got here?"

Oh, I have to tell you, Caroline is now a mum! But

more of that later or I shall completely lose my train of thought, such as it is. Jeff says my 'train' is still intact, it just runs on slightly different tracks to other people!

And the funniest thing of all is that a few months after all this happened, I was contacted by Circe Books from Atlanta, who had published my original story. Surely they didn't want me to write another one? I was done with writing, and soaps for that matter. Believe it or not, and this may sound bizarre to you coming from a woman closer to sixty than fifty, I am learning the cello. It drives Jeff mad because I take over his basement and he is forced to watch the hockey in the lounge. Ian is teaching me. He gave me William's cello as a memento and I couldn't bear to see it standing so forlorn and unplayed in a corner of the basement. So I asked Ian if he would teach me and, bless him, he jumped at the chance. I think it helps him deal with his grief, and Ian is so kind and patient, and says I have some talent. I know he is just being kind, but I do enjoy scraping away, and in the little time I have been learning I can already play three or four simple tunes. Ian says we will do a duet at Thanksgiving for the family. They are coming here this year. After mum died, Dad didn't want to stay on in Amelia by himself, so he is back now and in a lovely nursing home. I know we are supposed to call them senior assisted-communities but a bedpan by any other name. He loves it though. Although he can't get around much these days, he still has all his marbles, even at almost 95, and we visit him every few days and he comes to us whenever he wants, odd weekends, birthdays, holidays, you know the type of thing. He is the chess champion of The Maples (I know, not a very original name but they really are wonderful there). I remember when I went to see him a couple of months back and I noticed a little brass trophy on his bookshelf. "Gee Dad, what'd you win?"

"Aha! That! You are looking at The Maples grand chess champion, Kochanie!"

"Wow! Cool! Well done, Dad, I am proud of you!"

Dad started chuckling. "I only won because Max Schneider kept falling asleep between moves!" he grinned (with all his own teeth! Which is more than I can say for me, I am afraid!), "But what do you expect from a Kraut!"

"Dad!" I was outraged! But I could see his eyes smiling deliberately provoking me. Always the joker, always up to mischief, my dad. But I wanted to make my point, so I continued, "Dad, Max Schneider is Jewish and not even German. He's Swiss!"

Chuckling, Dad held up his hands in mock surrender.

"I know. I just love to make you mad! Max is my brother. We were born on the same day and his son, Morty, brings us in a bottle of Wyborowa when he is in town. We hide it from Nosey Nurse Nelly."

Nosey Nurse Nelly was actually Doctor Grace Ngoba, a beautiful and dedicated geriatric specialist, originally from Botswana. I kept meaning to find out how she ended up here in Ottawa as the chief medical officer in an upmarket old folks' home. I must ask her for dinner one evening. She is wonderful with Dad and he idolises her. Plus, she knows about the Polish vodka. When Max's son Morty brings it in, he gives the bottle to her and she dilutes it with about 80% water. But the illusion of illicit drinking remains and as Grace says, "If they behave like a couple of schoolboys, they have years left yet!"

Oh, sorry again! I was telling you about Circe Books. So, they didn't want another story, thank goodness. Well, not exactly. They wanted to write the story of my life! I could not for the life of me see what made my life so exceptional from everyone else that it would be worthy of a book and I certainly could name lots of much better candidates. It seems that they had called Sonya and Rachel to get a bit of background on me for their files as I had been a bit coy about telling a complete stranger my life story and Lord knows what those girls told them but they were very keen to write a book about me. I declined, of course. But they still want to send some reporter up to interview me. Let's keep our fingers crossed that they never get round to it. I have had a life more or less the same as most people, some good, some bad, so who would be interested in my story? It's not that exceptional. Oh I suppose losing my eye at eight might be slightly unusual but what is losing an eye to kids born without limbs or in wheelchairs or whatever, who overcome all sorts of horrors and adversity and triumph? No, I think they should stick to much more interesting subjects. But secretly, I admit, I am flattered.

Got to run, that's Ian at the door for my lesson! Trying a simplified bit of Chopin today. Well, I am half Polish!

★★★

It's funny, inside, I don't feel any different to the person I was that summer of the Montreal Olympics when I was just a kid doing a summer job at the Bay, but I am afraid the years are beginning to, well frankly, to be a pain in the bum! I am no longer willowy. In fact, the plant I most resemble these days is an aubergine! All the weight is in the bottom! Yes, a fat-arsed, shapeless aubergine. I know everyone here calls it an eggplant but my mum was from Pevensey in Sussex and over there they call them aubergines and that's what I learnt from her. Actually, like many Canadians, I am a bit schizophrenic when it comes to English. I say 'bum' or 'arse' rather than 'ass'. I always called my mother 'Mum' rather than 'Mom' but Paul's kids call Sarah "Mom". And don't get me started on miles and kilometres, or should that be kilometers! I spell colour with the 'u' and call gas, 'petrol'. But I call 'football', soccer and 'football' to me is CFL, our version, The Grey Cup not NFL and the Superbowl. So you see, it isn't easy being a Canadian! These days, the American version seems to prevail but anyone of my generation from British heritage can often find themselves falling between two stools!

Yes, Caroline is a mum, or a mom if you prefer! And

remember I talked about two births, well glory be if she didn't go and have twins! Just about the perfect everyday miracle! Girls, Heather and Elizabeth (after Mum, of course), five months old, born the day William died and a month after Mum and Ali, who left us in the same week. Mum had been failing for quite a while and Dad hated seeing her waste away. We had descended en masse the previous year for their platinum-anniversary party, which lasted about a week and the children all slept in tents, which was huge fun, while the adults took over the local motel about 100 yards up the road. All except poor Daniel and Caroline who were appointed tent monitors, one for the boys, one for the girls, and had to pitch camp with the kids! Jeffrey and I flew down a few days before the party to help get things organised. I wore a silver velvet patch this time because they don't do them in platinum! Paul was away on manoeuvres in the Atlantic somewhere but Caroline and Daniel had flown to Halifax and picked up Sarah and the two boys, Aaron and Bradley, and they came down together. What was fantastic was that Paul managed to organise a ship-to-shore call and got though just as the party was getting started and spoke to Granny and Granddad Wisniewski. Jake was there and both his girls, Jeannie and Samantha, flew in from out west with their husbands and children, which was a lovely surprise as most of us had never met their families. Mateusz turned up without Olga unfortunately as she had just had a mastectomy (happily, she is fine now) and stayed in Poland with Ela, their oldest daughter (who was pregnant for the fourth time), and baby Janusz and smaller baby Tomasz, but she insisted that Mateusz go. So Mateusz arrived in a maroon and white 1957 GMC bus which he bought on the Internet for $15,000 with his two boys, their wives and their six kids (three each) and his youngest daughter, Marina, her husband Grzegor, their two sons, Ela's husband, Andrew (who was originally from Cleveland), and their oldest girl, Matilda. He got everybody nametags, "in case the older folk were getting a bit hazy," he said looking at Jake and me. But it was a great idea as quite a few of us hadn't even met in person before, although, thanks to Facebook and Skype, we all kept up with varying degrees of regularity with the toings and froings, ups and downs of each other's lives.

Come to think of it, I suppose an extended family is a bit like having your own built-in soap opera. I mentioned that to Jeff. "Yes," he said, "but at least you can switch off the soaps!" Old cynic! In all, including the local friends and neighbours there were nearly forty people there and seventeen had arrived on the same bus! Everyone had such a wonderful time and mum was the centre of it all. She was already showing signs that she was ill but Dad said she didn't stop smiling for a week afterwards. When Mateusz and his clan returned to Poland he gave the bus to an orphanage in Jacksonville on condition that they gave him and the gang a lift to the airport!

But almost a year on from the party, it was coming to the point when some decisions about palliative care were going to have to be made when Mum, bless her, took the decision out of our hands. That was a grim couple of weeks; flying down to Amelia, staying a few days with Dad, who was much stronger than I would have been. He just said how lucky he felt to have shared so many years with someone so special and then dried his eyes and said, "OK, so find me a place in Ottawa and I'll be back soon." Jake flew down for the cremation (Dad wanted to bring Mum back to Canada and bury her there) and to stay on to help Dad sell up and move north. Obviously, Jake never retired to Amelia. He had a much more radical plan! So, Jeff and I flew back and gathered Sonya, Rachel and Larry, who were all staying at our house. Larry and Rachel, well, long story. Anyway we went off to Paris for Ali's funeral and it was only a couple of weeks after that that we were blessed with two more grandchildren.

It turns out that after dozens of tests and analyses, and years of heartbreak and despair, Caroline and Daniel decided to try and adopt. As part of the adoption process they both had to have a medical. And yes, implausible as it may sound, it was at her medical that the doctor asked if she was sure she wanted to go ahead with the adoption.

"Why on earth would you ask that?" asked Caroline half irritated, half perplexed.

"Well it's just that you know you are pregnant. About three months gone, I would say without a couple more tests."

Caroline screamed, jumped up and kissed Doctor

Patel full on the mouth (Doctor Patel was somewhat taken aback. No patient have ever upped and kissed her before!) and ran out of the examining room still in her robe to find Dan who was down the hall trying to pee into a cup!

Dan did try to explain to me how it had happened, something to do with his sperm becoming active again and Caroline's eggs deciding not to evacuate early. A combination of diet, herbal medicine, hormone injections and, in my opinion, divine intervention (although born and raised Catholic, neither Jeff nor I are churchgoers. Sorry, Sister Mary-Joseph, my long-suffering Sunday school teacher) resulted in two healthy miracles.

I will never forget the day they were born. We were at another hospital, Ian, Jeffrey, Rachel and I, (Larry was out of town on business and Sonya and Habib were still in their own bubble of grief) sitting around a bed covered with tubes, drips, monitors and the regular, crushingly depressing, bellows sound of the respiratory machine. Amongst that paraphernalia lay William. He had caught a chill at an open-air concert on the canal for, of all things, Breast Cancer Awareness Week. The chill developed into a severe cold, the cold into flu, and the flu into pneumonia. He fought it but after two months he had no more fight left and William, our sweet William, was a ghost. On that day William was drifting in and out of consciousness but unable to speak; we were all in tears when, with special permission from the duty nurse for me to leave it switched on (who had had William's consent granted by no more than a double blink), my cell phone rang: it was Daniel. "It's twins! Girls! Two gorgeous girls! Caroline wanted William to know." Just at that moment, William opened his eyes. I leaned in and kissed him, and told him he was an uncle. Despite his pain and the inevitability of his imminent death, William smiled and taking as firm a grip as he could of Ian's hand, he nodded and smiled again then closed his eyes. A few moments later, his hand slipped from Ian's and he was at peace.

***

So Jake decided to retire and, after Mum died and Dad returned to Ottawa, he, having abandoned the idea to live in Amelia, decided to make the most of his retirement. He went down to Portland, then to Boulder, to see his girls and his grandchildren, then came over to Ottawa to see Dad and stayed for a few days with Jeff and me. One evening, Ian joined us and we were sitting in the basement, with the cello banished to the corner, having a few cocktails. Well, we did have a cocktail bar and Ian could make a mean Manhattan! Jake had just turned sixty-six and was on his own, solvent from some astute oil investments back in the eighties, and he announced between sips that he had sold up and was moving onto phase three.

"What were phases one and two, may I ask?" I enquired.

"Phase one was youth...phase two was adulthood."

"So what is phase three, senility?" Jeff and Ian giggled. Jake snorted.

"Listen, Long John Silver," I stuck my tongue out at him. "Phase three is called 'Golden Time'. And I plan to make the most of it! And Dad knows all about it and he loves the idea!"

"What have you and that crazy old man been plotting?" Jeff asked.

"I am off to New Zealand. I am going to buy a plane and fly myself to Fiji and as many islands as I can!"

There were precisely three seconds of silence before Ian and Jeffrey fell about laughing. But I didn't laugh. I knew he was serious and I beamed. He got his pilot's licence twenty years before in Alberta and was an enthusiastic occasional club pilot. I got up went over to him and hugged him tight.

"I bet I know what Dad said when you told him."

"Yep. He said that it was about time there was another pilot in the family!"

Three weeks later we took Jake to Macdonald-Cartier airport and saw him off on the Air Canada flight to Vancouver where he would connect with Air New Zealand to Auckland. He had just one suitcase for the hold and a Canadian Army backpack as hand luggage and a grin on his face like that of a ten-year-old boy locked in a sweet shop. And that was that. Off he went and we get to Skype from time to time. He sailed through his medicals and got his New Zealand licence but has encountered the problem of finding a suitable single prop plane that had decent range. So, he took a commercial flight to Fiji and visited Tonga and a host of other islands. His plan has changed a bit but the Golden Phase seems to be even more gilt edged. He has a travelling companion; Karina, is Dutch, a widow of 59 and a former diplomat of all things, and seems as much of a lunatic as Jake! The new plan involves them going to Australia, buying a Cessna and hopping around the interior while their vineyard in Adelaide settles in! I cannot wait until we visit them next year! Mateusz has sold up too and he and Olga have bought two houses and knocked them into one on a small part of a big old estate for the brood, which now numbers twelve grandchildren. They plan to grow their own organic vegetables, enjoy fishing in the lake and entertaining the hordes when they descend upon them for the school holidays. The funniest thing is that the estate used to belong to a cousin of the Baron Karol, who taught my dad to fly back in the thirties. Dad was tickled when I told him. He never spoke to me in Polish. By the time I was born, he was so used to speaking English at work and to Mum that he never taught me. I sort of resented him a bit for that but at least I can insult people in Polish as he always cursed in his native tongue and I was a quick learner! But Jakey and Mat, being older, did learn it and when they speak on the phone, they speak in Polish, although you have to shout a bit these days as Dad's getting a trifle deaf.

Although I believe that his deafness is selective. Mum used to say, "Your father hears exactly what he wants to and not a word more!"

***

So, like I said, it has been an up and down couple of years. Well, like all my life, like all our lives it has had its fair share of good and bad, triumph and tragedy, or any other of those contrasts you can name. Ian bought a boat and plans to spend the winters in the Caribbean. He named it 'The Sweet William'. Jeff and I are swapping houses with Caroline, Daniel and the girls. They could use the space and we like their two bedroom apartment. It is in Sandy Hill, right back where we started; seems fitting somehow. Paul and Sarah have another baby on the way and have bought a pretty, old-colonial style house in Halifax and I just got a lovely email from Sonya and Habib. They are rushed off their feet with animals of all sorts which are brought in at all hours of the day and night. Habib calls the ranch, 'The Ark' and they are coming to visit this Thanksgiving and we are going there for Christmas.

So, you see, just as I said before, pretty standard stuff for a life. Certainly nothing worth putting in a book, but I am glad we had a chance to catch up.

Well, I better get going, Jeff is due home soon. He should have retired this year but they asked him to stay on to help settle the new guy in and he was happy to help. He has recently started curling; he calls it, "Bowls on ice for pensioners," but he takes it very seriously and I have a feeling I won't be seeing too much of him at weekends. But in a few months, I will have him around all week and Lord knows how that will work out!

***

Oh wait! I forgot. I wanted to tell you about Rachel and Larry! I remember telling you that they had a very bitter break up after 23 years of marriage. That was back in, let me see, it must have been 2003 or 2004, I think. Well, they had not been on speaking terms at all until their son Damien and his wife, Julie, had the triplets: Eve, Gillian and Tabitha. Well, after the girls were born, Larry and Rachel were civil to each other and spoke at family gatherings. Rachel went back into nursing and Larry stayed working with Jeff at Rogers. Rachel devoted herself to work and helping Julie with the girls and Larry went on a few middle-aged man type dates with younger women but nothing came of them.

Then just over two years ago, maybe a little less, Damien and Julie's house caught fire due to a short in the water heater of all things. Damien was out driving a cab, covering for one of his guys who had a burst appendix, and Julie and the girls who were about twelve at the time were asleep in bed. Fortunately, the smoke alarms worked and they all got out just in time. They lost everything and although the insurance covered most of it they were temporarily homeless. Larry offered for them to live at his house and said he would get a motel. Rachel was having none of that and insisted he stay at her apartment as long as he slept on the couch. That was all fine and while Damien and Julie were looking for a new place, Larry stayed with Rachel and they started hanging out like they were dating in college! Larry still slept on the couch but all the old rancour had gone and a genuine friendship was re-emerging. What pushed it from friendship back to true love was horrible.

It was the day that Damien, Julie and the girls were due to leave Larry's and move into their new house. Everyone was terribly excited and the girls were running in an out of Larry's house with boxes of clothes and bits of furniture that Larry was giving to them. Larry had mixed emotions because it meant leaving Rachel's and he felt rather flat about that. To tell the truth, Rachel felt the same but was too proud to admit it. Anyway, Tabitha, the youngest of the triplets by thirty-eight minutes, had a wooden-framed round mirror and was very gingerly taking her time carrying out to the van that Damien had hired. It wasn't heavy and Tab was being very careful. But she hadn't spotted that Evie had dropped a couple of coat hangers from her last trip to the van when loaded with winter coats. Somehow, Tabitha's foot got caught up in the hangers and she came crashing down with the mirror underneath her. She cut her wrists to ribbons and lost a lot of blood. The ambulance was there in four minutes and she was in the emergency room in twelve.

They gave her a transfusion and stabilised her and when she was out of danger, Damien and Julie started making the calls to let people know she was safe. But it was Larry who called me.

Since Rachel had called me earlier to tell me what happened I had been sick to my stomach. I wanted to go to the hospital or to Rachel's but she told me to stay put, as she may need someone to look after Eve and Gillian. So I waited by the phone chewing my nails and saying a prayer and apologising to Sister Mary-Joseph again. Towards evening, the phone rang and I snatched it up immediately. It was Larry. He told me she was fine but that when she fell, a sliver of glass from the mirror had gone into her eye and that it was too early to say what the prognosis was. I couldn't breathe. Suddenly the bus crash, the hospital, the little sleeping girl, Agatha, the doctors and nurses, my mum's 'Evening in Paris' perfume, the bandages, the names I was called by the girls at school and, most of all, the pale girl in the little mirror with the black patch came flooding back all at once. I had never had a bad dream about my eye or the accident in all those years but now it was as if the accumulated nightmares of fifty years had all come crashing down on me at once. I threw up on the breakfast bar. Larry was still on the phone and must have heard me sobbing and puking. Oh God!

"Nance, Nancy? Are you OK? Do you want me to bring Rachel over?"

I collected myself. "Don't be silly, Larry, I am fine.

All I care about is Tab right now. Promise you will let me know as soon as you hear anything?"

"Of course we will. You sure you ok, Hon?"

"Sure. Now go and make yourself useful. I am sure Damien and Julie could do with a break."

Well, medicine, particularly optical surgery, has improved out of all recognition since 1966. Micro-surgery and lasers and all sorts of things they have now. They got the glass out and saved the eye. Tabitha had to wear a patch for about three months while she healed but I leant her some of mine, and she ruled the school! Six months later Larry and Rachel got married again and I was a fifty-seven-year-old bridesmaid!

My patch matched my dress which Rachel had picked out... it was aubergine!

THE DINNER DATE

Denise: We have been married for eighteen years but tonight is only our third date! Personally, I blame Dr Phil and Oprah. And don't think it was my suggestion. It was Todd's daft idea. I always suspected that those days when he worked from home, all he did was goof off and watch TV.

In fact, a lot of our marriage has been the opposite of the conventional roles for men and women joined in that whole holy matrimony thing. But I am getting ahead of myself. Hello, I'm Denise Parkinson, née Driscoll, and I am English (or British as you say over here), born in Lincoln, forty-cough-years old, height: 5 feet five inches, weight: none of your damn business. Married to the aforementioned Todd and mother of two: Jane, eighteen (yes, the same age as the number of years we have been married), freshman at the University of Massachusetts, Amherst and Steven, sixteen, junior at Western High, Baltimore and part-time server at Subway, Charles Village outlet, on Saturdays and every other Sunday.

And I am sitting here in my office at Maryland Dream Realty (Get it? Where we make your dreams a Realty... sigh) at half past six on a Friday evening, putting on my make-up under strip lights with a powder compact mirror, showing only two square inches of my face at any one moment. My tights have a ladder and my black

Versace sequin stretch-wool cocktail dress is hanging on the doorknob. It has to stretch a little more than I would like but it is very cute and goes well with my LK Bennett Sledge leather court shoes, which I bought at Selfridges on our last trip to London to visit my sister, Harriet. Looks like I will have to go without tights, so good thing I shaved my legs this morning. I know I said we had opposite roles from convention, but that doesn't mean I stopped being a girl!

Anyway, I better get on with this mascara. The three whiskey sours I had at lunchtime and the doobie I lit up when everyone left about half an hour ago have all kicked in nicely and steadied my nerves for later but it's playing havoc with my make-up application! The office phone is direct to voicemail and I have my mobile on silent, so I reckon I have about twenty minutes before my 'date' gets here. He is always bloody early! I hope he gets stuck in traffic then I can have a fag and take a slug from Bob Carpenter's Wild Turkey – I know he keeps it in his filing cabinet. It should be a sackable offence but as I'm the boss, I will let it slide this time!

I can't believe I agreed to this. It's bad enough having to date your husband without him insisting we keep a bloody video blog of the sorry experience too. I think he wants to become a YouTube sensation. Well, Toddy boy, you asked for it 'warts and all'. Cheers, darling!

★★★

Todd: Hi! I just tried calling Den but she didn't pick up. I bet she is too psyched! This whole date thing has really got to her! I know she loves it. I knew she would as soon as I mentioned it to her when I saw that show on Lifestyle, *How to Keep it Alive: CPR for your marriage.* I was waiting for them to get us organized with a conference call with my boss in 'Frisco and our advertising guys in Chicago and I idly turned on the TV just as the piece on dating your spouse came up. And I thought, *Bingo!*

Hi! I'm Todd Parkinson. I live in Baltimore but I was born and raised in Falls Church, Virginia. I'm 48 and graduated GW in interior architecture, class of '88 and I'm a designer for an executive jet company. I design the interiors for your office in the sky. It's an election year in three years' time, so we are real busy right now gearing up for all those politicians' needs. I have been lucky enough to have been married to Denise for almost nineteen years and we have two beautiful children: Stevie, who is a catcher for his high school team, with a .380 batting average, and my very own princess, Janey, who is as cute as she is smart and has just started at Amherst. Stevie is almost seventeen and Jane turned eighteen last May. Yep, Den and I couldn't keep our hands off each other when we first met and although we were always going to get hitched. Janey helped us set the date, so to speak!

Jeez, it's almost quarter of seven, I better grab my coat and make a move! Den hates to be kept waiting. So long for now!

★★★

Denise: It's five past seven and darling Todd is, thankfully, stuck in traffic. He sent me a text: "Traf Nmare! B@U N20 X." I honestly think it takes longer to abbreviate text messages and render them nigh on incoherent than it would to compose them properly with correct grammar and punctuation. Well, it gives me the opportunity to have another cigarette which Todd strongly disapproves of and seems to enjoy lecturing me about and I'll just take another refreshing draft of Wild Turkey straight from the bottle. Is this my second or third? Oh well, doesn't matter, I can't face this date sober!

And not just a date, dear viewers, but a date with rules, no less! Fancy! My only rules for dating were to make sure I had clean panties on (unless he was really hot, had a decent car and looked like spending a fair bit on dinner in which case I would sometimes forego the panties altogether) and remember to put my diaphragm in my purse! I could have said 'knickers' instead of 'panties' and 'handbag' instead of 'purse' and, in fact, I switch between American English and British English depending on where I am and with whom I am talking. But the punters lap up the old Queen's English at work! I have been here in the States since I was eleven when Dad got offered a job as a professor at the University of Delaware, my alma mater, and left Mum and Harriet back in Lincoln. God, they were such socialists! So much so, that when they got divorced, they divided everything equally – even their daughters! But the olds have long croaked and Harriet is a PA in the city and although three years younger than me, she is a decided spinster. Actually, Hattie, if you ever get to see this, your sister thinks you're a lezza! Oh my! In vino, well, in Bourbon, veritas!

I shall have to reapply the lippy, mind. See Todd, smeared on the bottle and on my dog end?

So, the rules. We each get to ask the other six questions and we have to write down what we think the other will answer. But we don't know each other's questions beforehand and we have to video the other person as we ask them to catch the live reaction. How *Who's afraid of Virginia Woolf?* meets *Mr & Mrs*. I'd rather be soaking in the tub with a bottle of Chablis and maybe a line of coke then getting a massage from... well, I better stop there or I shall have to repair to the ladies again and I don't want to crease my Versace! Am I naughty? Do I shock you, Todd, and you, viewers? Well, if you knew what I know, you might not be so surprised that I am, well, how I am.

Bugger! He'll be here in a minute, so I better make sure I am ready to go. The other rule is that he takes us to Dino's Wine Bar before dinner where we walk in separately and we each have half an hour for a cocktail or two at either end of the bar like we're strangers. Then he 'picks me up' and we go to dinner at Zen. Three words; for fuck's sake! But who knows, I might get lucky in Dino's and have a great evening? Well, at least I have my questions ready and what I know will be his answers and I couldn't care less what he asks me although I bet I can guess. Now all I need to do is find my panties!

***

Todd: Hey! It's Todd again! I just sent a SMS to Den that I'm running late. But she didn't get back to me. I guess she must be getting ready for date night! And here I am, stuck in traffic behind a big rig with a blow out and rubber all over the freeway. Looks like I may be here for a little while. I hope she's not mad. She's been acting kinda funny lately; moody-like and bent outta shape over the littlest things. Sure, she always got cranky when she was on her period, but this has been going on a while. I guess it might be the menopause maybe. Anyway, Stevie is staying over with Jimmy Miller across the street playing Halo 4 or Rock Band 3 on Xbox so we have the place to ourselves when we get back. So, I suggested the dinner date to keep things fresh and keep Den sweet. It'll be cool, just like old times. We only ever had two proper dates before; our first date a couple of weeks after we met at that Christmas office party when I was breaking up with, oh what was her name now, Cherry or something like that. Anyway, this girl worked as a secretary and Den worked there too as file clerk at an attorney's in DC. And the second date led to Janey, so I must have been doing something right! What with the pregnancy and all, then the babies then work, you know how it is. Well we just never got to spend much time together as a couple and before ya know it, nearly twenty years goes by and you need to put the magic back!

Uh oh, looks like we're moving again. I better put the cam down. Don't want a ticket! Gee, that would be great on YouTube. Todd gets a ticket in a traffic jam!

Darn it! False alarm. We moved about ten feet! But should be any minute now. So, quickly, to tell you, we have devised some fun rules for our date. We each get six questions but can only ask them live at dinner and we each record the answers. I spent all yesterday thinking up my six and then I had to write down what I think Den's answers will be and we get to compare notes. Wanna hear my questions? Looks like I just have time.

OK, question one: do you remember we met?

I bet she says it was at the party when Cherry or whatever got real drunk because I told her we were through and Den, who had been watching me all night, came up to me and asked me if I was ok. Next thing I know she is kissing me like we were the world's greatest lovers. Man, she was hot! She was all over me and not even a bit hammered! I knew she had been checking me out all the while I was with Cherry. They were roommates and I had caught her coming out of the shower before, wearing nothing but a towel, so I figured it was only a matter of time. God, Den was hot back then; short skirts, tight tops and a great body. Even after kids and hitting 44, she still looks great when she gets herself done up. Sure, she has gained a few pounds, but in all the right places! Shame she has gone off a bit in the bedroom department. I guess it must be the menopause. But I don't mind that much. I know we can find our spark again. She started taking yoga classes on a Tuesday and Thursday evening for a while, a few years back, and I thought she was trying to get less stressed so that we could relax again and have fun in the sack like we used to. But didn't seem to help at all. Although she always enjoyed the classes and came back looking relaxed, but then just took a bath and slept like a baby! Then last year she tried photography, going over to my cousin, Hannah's place on Saturdays. Hannah is a professional portrait photographer. Den really enjoyed it, although I never saw her stuff. She says it was private, like a diary and just to help her keep her centred and focused. I have no idea what that means but she seemed to enjoy it. She dropped it though, just like the yoga, when Hannah sold her studio and went to Paris to work with some famous chick in a photographic gallery.

Question two: what has been the happiest moment of your life?

Well, that's a no-brainer really. Gotta be the birth of our amazing kids. Both just popped out, no fuss at all! And they are the light of our lives. It is just a tragedy that we lost one in between, a daughter, when poor Den was nearly six months gone.

OK, this time we really are just about to move, so I'm gonna go and my other four questions will just have to be a surprise for dinner. When we get to Dino's, we are going to pretend like we don't know each other, then

I will go over to her and pick her up! Cool, huh? I bet that will turn her on, having a dude just walk up to a more mature lady as if she is the hottest girl in the place. But, mister, I am telling you, she probably will be. My true, true sweetheart has still got it!

★★★

Denise: Still no sign of my hot date – glory be! The Wild Turkey is a dead duck and I have what they call over here, a bit of a buzz! Good. Anything that helps me make it through the evening. So, while I am waiting for Prince Charming, the love of my life (ha!) and father of my children (well one for sure!), I suppose I better go through my questions. Now where did I jot them down, somewhere in my purse... oh here they are; I scribbled the first four down on a torn outside of a carton of maxi pads. I've been as regular as clockwork since I was twelve and half – you can set your watch by my time of the month! That's how I knew I was pregnant all four times within a couple of weeks. Oops! Little kitty, back in the bag! Well, Todd, you know about three of them; our living children and the one in between them, the little girl that never saw the light of day... poor mite. Accidentally falling down the stairs is never good in your second trimester, is it? I know I shouldn't have been drinking, but I only had one glass of wine to take up to bed and keep me company while I was finishing my revision for my realtor's exams. But it hit me like a freight train and

91

I just couldn't tell where the top step was and sort of guessed; I lost my balance and fell backwards all the way down. And you, dead to the world and snoring like a pig, didn't find me until morning when I was lying in a pool of blood at the foot of the staircase. I was too ashamed to tell the doctor I had been drinking and he was too sensitive to bring it up. I still remember what you said to me when you got to the hospital after dropping Jane off at the child-minder's: "It's OK, Den, honey. We can try for another as soon as you are better." And my God, how you tried starting within a week of me getting out of hospital. But three months later, my period clock told me that these 'efforts' had paid off and almost a year to the day after the miscarriage, our son, Steven, made you the proudest father in the world and left me so exhausted that I couldn't feed him for three months. The hospital found us that Mexican wet nurse, Jacinta (whose own baby was stillborn), who came to live with us until I was strong enough for the baby. Such a sweet girl, only seventeen, and she was great with the children. Strange her leaving in the middle of the night like that. Her note was in Spanish and I took it to the office to get Javier, the janitor, to translate it: Jacinta had been warned by a friend that the INS were about to visit all the houses in our neighbourhood as part of a crackdown on illegal domestic staff. I was better by then, but I would have liked to say goodbye.

Yes, Toddy, I have been pregnant four times. The fourth, which was actually my first, you don't know about. Nobody knows about it. I lost it within a few weeks and the father is long gone. Besides, he never knew. And don't worry, I was teasing, Steven is your son, I can guarantee it. After all, once I got out of hospital, I never left the house for three months and I am sure no one else raped me within three months of miscarrying, did they?

You set the rules for our date video blog: film the before, during and after. And if nothing else, a blog should tell the truth, shouldn't it, Todd? And in keeping with the rules, here are my questions for you and I already know how you will answer so I will film my own interview. When I have the camera on my left, like now, I am me, asking, and on the right, like so, I am you, answering.

Ahem, so, Todd, darling,

Q. What made you come up with the idea of videoing the date.?

A. "I just thought it would be a cute keepsake and something for fun for our friends to see on YouTube."

(He will be totally sincere when he says that. It'll make him feel safe. We are in it together and I am playing the game.)

Q. What do you all day when you are working from home?

A. "I work, make calls, do my designs. Sure, I take a break now and then and watch a little CNN."

(He'll tell a little white lie. He looks at porn on the internet and watches the fashion channel for the swimsuit shows I suspect. But it's not a hanging offence.)

Q. Did you enjoy being a stay-at-home dad?

A. I loved every minute of it. I knew you were busy with your career so I figured the best way to support you was to do as much as I could with the kids.

(Yes, I only found out just how much he enjoyed it a few days ago.)

Q. If we had never had children, would we still be married?

A. How can you ask that? Of course, you're my true, true sweetheart!

He first called me his 'true, true sweetheart' when he raped me for the third or fourth time when I was pregnant with Jane. It was his little nickname for me, grunting out the words as he pounded into my body wherever and however he wanted. At least he didn't tie me up, use the belt, burn me with cigars or use objects like bottles on me when I was pregnant. How was I to know? I fell pregnant the second time we went out on a date and after all that I had been through before, I couldn't lose another baby that way, so how else could I survive? I would have been a single mother on a junior secretary's salary with so much debt from college, even though I dropped out after two years, and of course, Sheryl had kicked me out when she found out her boyfriend of six months had knocked up her roommate. So when I knew I was pregnant, Todd, you did the 'honourable' thing and got down on one knee in the Seven Eleven and asked me to marry you. What choice did I have? And looking back after all these years, it has just occurred to me, talking to this JVC camcorder, that I think that's how you hoped it would go; that you would get a desperate, sad and lonely girl so dependent on you, that you could do what you liked to her, whenever you wanted. A girl, so alone and vulnerable, with a history of promiscuity and substance abuse, that you could use her as a toy. And you did, didn't you, Todd? And you convinced yourself that it was what I really craved, that I liked it rough and kinky that I had thrown myself at you like a damsel in distress swoons before a knight in shining armour. I honestly believe that you have repeated that myth to yourself so many times, that it is your reality. I bet you would even pass a lie detector test about it... but maybe not about Jacinta, eh Todd? And, not about Jane either.

I know how he will answer my last two questions too; the first one will be a one word answer to the longest question he has ever been asked and he won't get a chance to answer the final question. But I am saving those until we get there!

★★★

Todd: Great dinner wasn't it my true, true sweetheart? OK, here we are just enjoying a brandy after an excellent dinner and now it's... drum roll please... question time! Ready, Den? OK, like we agreed, I go first. So if you will just look into the camera please, Miss, and answer in your own time.

Question one, for the toaster oven! Ha, ha! Just kidding! OK. Question one: do you remember how we met?

And just wait until I get you in focus, ok, go!

Denise: Yes. At a Christmas party at Eastman and Tate where Sheryl and I worked as secretaries. You were shagging her but she got wasted and passed out on the toilet floor after throwing up and you grabbed my arse and stuck your tongue down my throat and I was drunk and high enough to let you. Next question please... no comments until after my final question, remember, Todd? Your rules, hon... next question please.

Todd: Err, question two: what has been the happiest day of your life?

Denise: What's the matter, Todd, not enjoying your date? Listen, babe, I am playing by the rules, your rules. Err, camera on me please! The answer is today could be the start of the happiest days of my life.

Todd: Den please, quit kidding around... ok, ok don't get up... Question er... three.

Yes, three... do you have any regrets?

Denis: Yes. I should have had the duck paté as a starter; the feta salad was too salty. Next... I said next, Todd.

Todd: Look, Den, I don't know what's gotten into you lately so let's forget it and go home, ok?

Denise: Oh no, Todd, darling! I am having too much fun this was *such* a great idea of yours. Let's carry on? No? Well if you have finished, I think it only fair to ask my questions. Actually upon reflection, I only have two. The first one is – look at the camera, Todd, please – the first question is in several parts and is quite long, so focus, honey, focus... my first question is:

What would you say if I told you I didn't love you, never have and that I have had two affairs: one with my yoga instructor, Nadine, and the other with your cousin Hannah because every time you or any man touches me now, I want to die? And that I know you raped Jacinta and made her write that ridiculous runaway note and that I want a divorce and if you ever come near me, Steven or Jane, especially Jane, I will kill you? Wait, I haven't finished, sit down!

I only figured it all out last week when you suggested date night and told me the rules and gave me the camera. Why now? I asked myself. Why after leaving me alone for the last three years? Then it hit me like a sledgehammer and after I got over being sick, I started to act. I called Jane at college and we talked for four hours on the phone. She went to the counsellor on Wednesday and they are waiting for me to get there tomorrow with Steven, who is at a motel with the Millers where they are all waiting for me. God, I am so stupid! I will never forgive myself for not knowing or suspecting and poor Jane was too scared to tell me. She didn't want you to do to her what she heard you doing to me all those years. And you were so kind to her showering her with love and praise and support, your 'princess'! She was too young to understand and I was too busy staying at work to keep away from you. Jane is safe from you now and I am going up to Amherst in the morning to stay with her for a few days and I am taking Steven with me. The police will hear everything about how you raped and beat me for the first fifteen years of our marriage, about how you drugged me when I was pregnant with another baby girl because you wanted a son an heir and pretended to be asleep while I lay bleeding in agony on the floor while my little girl died inside me and I will tell them why you were suddenly fine with no longer forcing yourself on me after fifteen years of abuse, because you had a new target in your sights, my daughter Jane; my beautiful, sweet, clever girl. And if you want to know why I was such a slut, why I prefer women, why I want to kill you right this second more than anything in the world? It's because my other pregnancy, which ended in an illegal abortion and me nearly dying of septicaemia, the one you don't know about happened, when I was twelve and the father was my own father. So you see, Todd, I know your game it has been played before but you have made your last move. So what are you going to do?

Todd: *Den!*

Denise: And why do you keep bloody calling me 'Den' after all these years when you know how much I hate it? That was my last question. Now smile for the camera and I will be on my way. Thanks for the date, Todd.

***

Denise: Well, I have got used to this video blogging now so for those of you who saw the TV reports, let me just fill you in on how we all are now, eighteen months on from the dinner date.

Jane is still going to counselling but she is a strong girl, and has stuck with school and volunteers at the children's hospital at the weekends. She is going to major in psychology and wants to work with abused children and she only has nightmares every now and then. Bryan, her boyfriend is so patient and supportive and gentle, not to mention good-looking, I think Jane is going to be alright. Steven starts here at Amherst in the fall and we live about thirty miles from the college so he and Jane see a lot of each other. He may even get a baseball scholarship. I got a transfer to Massachusetts Dream Realty and am managing three branches and am happily single and definitely not dating anyone, I am also clean and sober and have been since that night.

They arrested and arraigned Todd on multiple charges. But he got lucky. He was knifed in the neck while in custody and bled to death in about two minutes. The guard said he would have got to him sooner but he dropped his key and by the time he had retrieved it and reached Todd, it was too late.

I must dash now, I have two more meetings this afternoon then Jane and Bryan are coming over for pot roast. Toodle pip until next time!

A GOOD TEACUP

It was a bit cracked, but it was good teacup. The glaze was threaded with the spider's web of tiny imperfections and the memories of many cups of tea. Tea and sympathy, tea and cake, high tea, a hot cuppa, tea-times uncountable from the morning brew to the late-night infusion. With milk, with lemon, with honey and even with a wee drop of something stronger – the cup had seen it all.

English Breakfast, Caravan, Earl Grey.

I looked out of the window as the winter night inexorably, inevitably slid into the grey murk of a December morning. A watched kettle never boils, so they say, but it always does. A watched dawn never breaks. That is sometimes true. December dawns do not break with that glorious brilliance of the first rays of a golden morning. Rather, they slink guiltily into the sky as if they know that they are something of a disappointment.

I glanced over at the battered stainless-steel saucepan, monitoring the boiling process as a solicitous doctor might glance at his patient's chart. It was a simple thing that I was doing; making a cup of tea to bring to the woman who was softly sleeping in the bedroom. Thousands, maybe millions of people were doing the

101

very same thing at the very same moment. But to me, this morning, it was significant. It was special. It was the first time she had stayed overnight. It was the first time we had fallen asleep in each other's arms. And this, this was to be the first cup of tea that I would bring to her in bed.

Lapsang Souchong, Assam, Dimbula.

We had bought the cup the afternoon before. It was shamelessly cold, the wind enjoying itself as it bit icily into the rush of Christmas shoppers struggling with packages and parcels, bags and boxes. A woman, wrapped in so many layers of winter clothes that they limited her movement and who was additionally encumbered by six or seven plastic carrier bags in one hand while grimly clinging on to her similarly swaddled child with the other, struggled up the slope of the street, like a weary salmon against the stream of pedestrians whose only objective, so it must have seemed to her was to hinder her progress. A milky light spilled over the threshold of the little bric-a-bracerie as its door opened and a customer hurried out onto the pavement. Just to get out of the grip of the chill, albeit for but a moment, we stepped inside.

The owner of this charming jumble of a shop, which was something between an antiques' emporium, a junk-shop, a boutique of curiosities, a flea-market, and a rather dusty Aladdin's cave, was exactly as he should be. Not old but ageing, no longer lithe but not creaking. Rather like a favourite pair of shoes, he was worn with time but had a fair number of good solid years left yet. His face was somewhat lived-in but seemed comfortable with the passing of the years. He was outwardly a little gruff, a little rough, but his eyes were clever, bright and although you wouldn't describe him as kind and gentle, he was, to be a little old-fashioned, a decent sort. While we chatted amiably together for a few minutes, I warmed my semi-frozen behind in front of the large electric-bar fire. She spotted the cup; large, grimy but with a pleasing shape and a nicely heavy weight. It was indeed, a little cracked. "But it's a good teacup," she said. We bought it, said our goodbyes and merry Christmases and plunged back into the icy current of the sodium-lit street.

Yunnan, Keemun, Shanghai Rose.

We stumbled into the flat, numb and pink with cold, and light-headed with the intoxication of each other. Laughing and kissing we tugged and pulled, unbuttoned and unzipped, shuffled and kicked our way from the hall to the bedroom, leaving a breadcrumb-trail of our clothes, mixed and dispersed, so that we amorous Hansels and Gretels might find the way out again. We made love. Urgently, boisterously then languidly, luxuriously. Then we ate a little, then we slept.

Darjeeling, Oolong, Ceylon Orange Pekoe.

And now, the water was beginning to boil and I watched the bubbles play and slap the sides of the pan for a few moments. This was what I had been dreaming of for months. It wasn't the holding hands, shyly at first then more boldly. Nor the thrill of the first stolen kiss, nor the rather awkward fumblings of foolish adults getting to know each other's contours, nor even the first magical, primal, beautiful, funny, passionate, slightly self-conscious but just lovely occasion when we first made love. It was now, the morning after she had slept in my arms for the first time, bringing her a cup of tea in bed. This had been my dream. I spelt out her name in the condensation on the window as I let the tea brew, and I glanced down at the street below where the last-minute, desperate Christmas Eve shoppers were setting off for the final battle. I wished them all good luck, picked up the steaming teacup and went back to the bedroom. She was just waking up and stretching and making those little noises that accompany such an activity. She sat up and smiled at me. She was beautiful.

"Good morning, my love. I brought you a cup of tea."

HARPER

Harper didn't look at the face of the man who was about to shoot him. He had always imagined that when staring death in the face, one would look at the face of the harbinger itself. Harper was surprised that he felt no terror or anguish about the prospect of his imminent and violent demise. In fact, he felt more vexed that he was about to die without having done so many of the things that he had dreamed of doing. He felt rather angry that the about-to-be murderer was so inconsiderate of the plans he had made for the next few years and most of all, he felt a mild curiosity about the fact that he was not looking at the assassin's face, which was unmasked and just a few feet above where Harper knelt on the dirty garage floor, his hands clasped above his head. He wasn't even looking at the dull, black 9mm Glock, which he remembered was Austrian and had a magazine capacity of seventeen bullets. Then he asked himself why this piece of trivia should pop into his brain at such a moment and decided it was probably a distraction mechanism, to deflect his attention from adjacent doom. What he was looking at with almost complete absorption and utter fascination was the stitching on the black glove of the hand holding the pistol. The glove was not particularly remarkable, almost certainly genuine leather but the stitching had become a little worn in one place on the second knuckle of the ring-finger and one stitch had worked itself partly loose and looped up from the glove leaving the tiniest of gaps between the thread and the leather. It was through this tiny eyelet that Harper concentrated his gaze as if seeing what was on the other side was all that mattered, temporarily oblivious to his predicament.

***

I wish he would get on with it already, Harper thought to himself. *My knees are killing me!* Still the gloved hand held the gun a few inches from Harper's forehead and Harper noticed that the gloved hand was rock steady. *Obviously a professional,* he thought to himself. If it had been Harper about to kill someone, he felt sure he would have been shaking like a leaf and, when it came to it, he couldn't have pulled the trigger no matter what the motivation to do so.

Harper considered trying to plead his case all over again, to say for the hundredth time that it was all a case of mistaken identity that whoever they were after, it wasn't him. Maybe he looked like the chap or had a similar name but whatever someone had seen, said or done to warrant such a grisly end in an abandoned garage in a dingy northern Paris suburb, that someone wasn't Harper. He was about to open his mouth but he changed his mind. Frankly, the whole thing was becoming rather a bore. Why didn't the bastard shoot? Although the hand holding the gun did not waver a millimetre, Harper sensed something was holding the killer back. *Definitely not conscience*, Harper reflected, *but what then? Doubt?* Maybe he was going over all the protestations of innocence that Harper had babbled in the preceding two hours when he was snatched off the quiet side-street in broad daylight and subjected to a very uncomfortable car ride, mostly face down in the back of a Peugeot, what was it, a 407? The saloon one anyway, the one that junior executives get whose grade doesn't qualify for a BMW yet, not even if they pay the difference to go up a grade. Again, Harper marvelled at his own capacity for trivia, particularly at such a time. In the two hours or so since the man had come up to him and stuck the pistol in his back and just said one word, "Marche," he had uttered not a word. The same was true of the driver. All Harper had seen of him was the greasy brown hair poking out from a blue and white toque, which looked like it had been knitted by an elderly female relative, and the reflection of his watery blue eyes and unkempt brows in the rear-view mirror. The fact he hadn't been blindfolded or hooded, Harper took to be a very bad sign indeed.

Whatever the hesitation was, it now appeared to be past as Harper saw the fingers on the pistol move slightly as if the man holding the gun were making sure of his grip. Harper closed his eyes and felt no more than vague disappointment that his entire life was not flashing before him in a super fast-forwarded special-effect moment. There was no cocking of the pistol. The Glock is an automatic. You just squeeze gently on the trigger. Harper heard the other man take a deep breath and hold it. He did the same. The maddeningly annoying, tinny chimes of the Nokia ringtone surprised both of them.

★★★

Harper had spent his first few days in Paris in a sort of happy trance. His French was decidedly average but he always accompanied every foray into the Gallic tongue with such a disarming smile and deference that even the usually contemptuous shop assistants and petty officials who seemed to make up most of the people he met, warmed to him and were, for the most part, amazingly helpful. Harper had had the foresight to arrange his accommodation via the internet through an experienced firm of professional relocation specialists before leaving England rather than brave the jungle of private ads or local estate agents who demanded such an assortment of documents and guarantees that many less fortunate flat-seekers had despaired and given up. After his girlfriend of seven years, Miranda had moved out and up (she was now dating a minor marquis), he had let his flat in Fulham and the rent more than covered the mortgage. He took voluntary redundancy, which was just as well because at thirty-eight, he already felt past it in the world of ethical commodity trading, (especially when they introduced him to his new boss, Sian, a twenty-six-year-old half American, half Welsh MBA with dreadlocks and a tattoo of a satyr doing unspeakable things to an angel on her permanently exposed shoulders and whose father was the major shareholder in the company), and the generous payment that went with it and had set off for Paris to write a book about a witty, charming sales executive who gives it all up to go to Paris to write a book. Not original, perhaps, but it was his dream and he had enough money not to worry about work for a while. He had inherited a reasonably profitable portfolio from his thrifty and prudent Scottish grandfather and if he was not too extravagant, Harper figured he could live modestly for quite a few years and even then, he could always sell the flat.

After two months, he had established a pleasant routine. He would get up early and plunge into the shower, then run down the stairs three at a time before emerging onto the Rue Rivoli, crossing the river at the Pont Neuf and having coffee and pain au chocolat at a little café on the Isle de la Cité. Sometimes picking up a few groceries on the way home, Harper would bound up the stairs, again three at a time, well, until the fourth floor after which the bounding slowed to a trudge, and spend an hour or so reading or dealing with any correspondence. Loathing email except for work or administrative related matters, Harper preferred to write long letters on good quality paper with a fountain pen. He always believed that it was more personal and that he crafted his missives with more attention than simply tapping out the equivalent of an electronic postcard to the people he cared about.

After that, Harper would take his orange and red Oxford lined A4 writing pad and a few ball-points (refilling fountain pens when out and about being rather a nuisance) and head off for either the Tuileries or the Jardin de Luxembourg, if the weather was dry, or one of the famous cafes like the Zimmer or the Sarah Bernhardt if it was wet. He would take up residence in one of the comfortable green metal slatted chairs strewn about the parks or in a plush red velvet booth in the Zimmer, and chewing absent-mindedly on the pen top, he would set to writing. Often he came up with whole paragraphs, sometimes just a few sentences or even individual words and often the mental wanderings manifested themselves in the form of doodles, scribbles and other undecipherable scrawls. Some days there would be nothing more than just lists. Harper liked making lists. Lists of his favourite films (the top three at that moment being *The Third Man*, *The Jungle Book* and *North by Northwest*) or the number of Capital cities he had visited (seventeen) or his former 'girlfriends' (he wasn't totally sure but he thought six if you count snogging Ingrid Spencer at the Youth Club disco when he was thirteen and a one night stand with a slightly drunk Bulgarian girl he had met inter-railing in Zurich and who, to his shock and dismay, had demanded three hundred Swiss Francs the next morning as payment for services rendered).

Skipping lunch if he was in a park, or ordering a sandwich and a small glass of red wine or a Kir in a café, Harper would pack up his tools around five o'clock in the afternoon and take a wander around the Latin Quarter to watch the world go by and to browse in one of the many little curio boutiques and bookshops in the area. Often, he would call in at the cramped treasure trove of an English book store, run by a somewhat cynical and diffident, yet gracious and charming, Canadian woman called Lisa, who had arrived in Paris twenty years earlier on holiday and somehow forgot to go home. Lisa had married well and divorced better and was always colourfully dressed like a rich woman's idea of a gypsy. She was around forty-five and lived with her Mexican girlfriend, Inez, who taught Spanish at the Sorbonne by day and the Tango at a little club in the 19th Arrondissement at the weekends. Harper would stop by for half an hour or so and drink a few cups of coffee with maple syrup and chat to Lisa who was an absolute mine of useful local information from the best dry-cleaner to where to find the essential expat products such as PG Tips, Coleman's Mustard and Bassets Liquorice Allsorts. Inez would sometimes be there. She was strikingly beautiful with jet-black hair in a plait to her waist and looked the epitome of a leading lady from a *Zorro* film. Harper was half in love with her, as were many men and women. But Inez only had eyes for Lisa and the two of them had been together for ten years and shared an oddly decorated yet welcoming three-room apartment nearby with two ageing stray cats.

By seven, Harper was usually hungry and returning home, he would make himself something to eat, unless he accepted a rare invitation to dinner. He hadn't yet entertained anyone at his place partly because he was still finding his feet and partly because he was enjoying the solitude. Thanks to the patient instruction of Lisa and Inez, he had a rapidly expanding repertoire of dishes which had gone from a baguette and cheese and maybe a few olives to elaborate salads, salmon in almond sauce and chicken à la king in just a few weeks. Harper hadn't smoked since he was a student apart from a very occasional cigar but he did like a drop of wine. He would drink a couple of glasses with dinner then he would spend an hour or so typing what he had written that day into his laptop.

At ten, he might go out again for a nightcap and find a quiet or lively café (depending on his mood) with or without people he knew. He had met a few people at the bookshop and most of them were permanent expats who used the bookshop more or less as an unofficial social club; a place to chat, drink coffee and moan about the French, which is the favourite pastime of foreigners in Paris. Harper had met few French people but one couple, Patrick and Helene Bernard, who worked for a satellite TV station and who lived in his building, had invited him for dinner one night and seemed to have taken on the responsibility for finding him a French girlfriend to improve his knowledge of the language and culture.

Consequently, that very evening he was due to meet

the Bernards for an apéro and they had invited, "A simply lovely girl, Audrey. She works in the news department and *elle est charmante* and she will just love you," the Bernards had enthused.

★★★

Both men looked somewhat irritated and bemused by this Finnish musical interruption to the serious business of murder at hand. Harper suddenly felt like giggling but thought better of it when he opened his eyes and saw the Glock still levelled at his forehead. Harper knew it wasn't his phone since his had some nondescript, jazzy factory preset, which he had yet to work out how to change. Besides, it had been switched off when the man had taken it off him when he bundled him into the car along with his wallet and his Oxford writing pad, which now lay in shreds in the corner of the filthy garage illuminated by a single, naked, low-wattage light bulb. Angrily and without lowering the pistol, the assassin reached into his inside coat pocket with his free hand and with some difficulty, encumbered by his glove as he was, extracted the still ringing mobile. Not taking his eyes off Harper for an instant, he pressed a button and holding the phone to his ear, he didn't utter a word of greeting. He listened for a full minute with no change of expression on his expressionless face and finally grunted, "D'accord," into the phone before pressing another button and thrusting the phone into a side pocket of his navy trench coat which, given the struggle he had had to withdraw it from its original interior pocket, seemed the easiest course of action.

Still looking intently at Harper, he slowly shook his head, then closing one eye he extended the hand holding the pistol to its full extent until the end of the barrel was pressing lightly into Harper's forehead. Harper kept his eyes open this time and again, found his mind sidetracked from his certain and immediate death to being slightly surprised that the gun metal did not feel as cold as he had imagined.

"*Fermez les yeux*. Your heyes, cloze zem, please," said the man in a dull monotone. *At least he's polite, he said please*, thought Harper and then wished he had thought of something more profound and revelatory since it was to be his final thought.

He felt a blow, like a hammer, against his skull and blinding, flashing lights splintered like a million fireworks in his brain and he felt no more.

★★★

The Bernards were bustling about their apartment two floors below Harper's flat getting things ready for the evening ahead. Patrick had already opened a bottle of Chateauneuf du Pape and was busy uncorking a nicely chilled Chablis. Helene Bernard was laying the table with various tasty morsels such as olives stuffed with feta cheese, avocado dip and a dozen fresh oysters she had picked up on the way home from work at the Place des Ternes. Audrey was due in thirty minutes at seven-thirty. Helene had invited her half an hour before the time they had agreed with Harper because she wanted to give her a full brief on her prospective English beau and to ply her with a glass or two to slightly loosen her inhibitions. Audrey was a good-looking, intelligent woman of thirty who had a tendency to be rather severe with men since she had spent most of her adolescence and adulthood fighting off their, largely, unwanted attentions. She had scared off most of the self-styled eligible bachelors and all of the married men at the office and wasn't looking for a man. However, Audrey was a romantic at heart and believed that she would meet someone when she least expected it and so never went looking. Patrick and Helene loved her like a sister and had determined to find her a decent man. Why they felt the need to act as matchmaker to the people they cared for was rather a mystery but Helene suspected it was because, unable to have children themselves, they sought and found vicarious pleasure in trying to bring about the happiness of their friends. And, unusually for modern day matchmakers, they were incredibly successful. So far, even the would-be romances that they had tried to bring about which never came to be had always ended in friendship and not once had they had to face any unpleasant fallout from their well-intentioned meddling. They cared deeply for Audrey and they had found Harper delightful, elegant, lonely and immensely engaging, and Helene thought him dashingly handsome without a trace of vanity. He wasn't looking for a wife, a lover or a mother, or, the usual dream woman for a Parisian man, a combination of the three. Harper was happy being in Paris and enjoying his new found freedom and both Patrick and Helene were sure that he and Audrey would hit it off.

At ten past seven, the buzzer sounded at the door. It was the doorbell to the apartment and not the buzzer on the street, so that meant either it had to be one of the building residents or perhaps Audrey arriving early as she knew the door code. But arriving early in Paris was unheard of. Slightly puzzled, Patrick set down the bottle of Chablis as it gently sweated condensation and went to the door. One of the guests was early.

***

Harper fell over the threshold and collapsed unconscious on the floor of the narrow, harlequin-tiled hallway. He had blood oozing from a nasty looking gash above his right temple. Helene gave a little scream but at the same moment reached for the phone on the cherry wood table by the door and dialled for an ambulance. Patrick, who had served for three years in the navy and knew a thing or two about not panicking and treating wounds, didn't try to move Harper who had twisted as he had fallen and was half on his side. Patrick, as gently as if he were handling a newborn chick, manoeuvred the prone figure into the recovery position and went to fetch some ice to hold against the wound. Finding that the remaining ice had been used up for the oysters, he grabbed the bottle of Chablis, which still had the corkscrew in it and wrapping it in a tea-towel held it against the crimson soaked temple of the unconscious man.

The ambulance arrived within ten minutes. By that time Harper, feeling sick and looking paler than Darius, one of Lisa's cats who was a true albino, had regained painful consciousness and was trying to recollect who he was and how he had got to be lying on the floor of these nice people's flat with blood all over his face.

Audrey, dressed in a black and white striped light-woollen dress with her hair up in a careless yet elegant chignon arrived just as the paramedics were taking Harper out on a stretcher. Ever the gracious hosts, Patrick and Helene delayed the extraction of the victim for a few moments as they effected introductions.

Harper managed a crooked smile and a slightly slurred, "Enchanté," before slipping comfortably back onto the stretcher and into painless oblivion.

★★★

Harper was back on his feet and out of hospital the next day. He sported an impressive rainbow-coloured black eye and several stitches, and was almost disappointed when the doctor told him that he wouldn't have a scar. He told the doctors at the hospital and the concerned Patrick, who had insisted on coming in the ambulance with him, that he couldn't remember what had happened but he thought that he had probably been mugged and had his phone and wallet stolen by someone who had hit him from behind, since he didn't remember seeing anyone.

He gave the briefest of statements to a rather grave young police officer, who spoke surprisingly good English, who told him that it was very unfortunate but since Harper could not remember seeing his attacker or attackers, there was little the police could do except to sympathise. Harper thanked the officer for his kind words and repeated the mugging story to Patrick, and later the following evening again to Helene, and yet again to Audrey a few days after that when the four of them gathered in the Bernards' apartment for dinner.

Several months passed in a most pleasant fashion as Harper was not plagued by nightmares about his all too near-death experience and he resumed writing his book, enjoying his surroundings and rapidly improving his French, thanks to seeing Audrey on a very regular basis. They weren't exactly an item, but they were happy and relaxed in each other's company and, according to the contented and not dispassionate opinion of Helene, it was only a matter of time before they would become an official couple.

One murky and drizzly autumn evening, Harper was walking along the Seine on the Quai aux Fleurs, near Notre Dame, with a bottle of champagne in one hand and a carrier bag full to the seams with raspberries, mushrooms and fresh shrimps in the other. He was going to attempt his most ambitious meal yet. He was making dinner for Audrey, who had become an occasional overnight guest at his flat, and tonight it was her saint's day, which serves as a sort of unofficial second birthday for many Catholics, even non-practising ones, since it is a splendid excuse for a party. Harper had consulted with Inez and Lisa and was going to make a champagne, shrimp and mushroom pasta with shallots and parsley and a raspberry and champagne sorbet for dessert. He was whistling softly as he sauntered along and trying not to feel too pleased with himself.

He stopped to cross the street when he felt a sudden, firm pressure in the small of his back. His mouth went dry, his scalp prickled with sweat and he clutched onto the champagne bottle and the carrier bag handle as tightly as he could. *Not again! Please, no! Had the assassin returned to finish the job this time?*

"Please do not turn round, mon ami." *It was the same expressionless voice, yet still polite,* Harper thought, his coping mechanism of concentrating on the minutiae of the man's manners having kicked in.

"I know you 'ave said nossing to zi police. Zat is good. I am very sorry about it all. You were not ze right person. Please forgive me and you shall not 'ave any more problem from me again. Now, I ask you to stay where you are and count to twenty. Merci."

Harper felt the pressure on his lower back disappear, and try as he might he heard nothing. He closed his eyes and counted to twenty, aloud and slowly. As he reached twenty, he opened his eyes again and without looking round, took a deep breath and crossed the road and went back to his flat. When he unpacked the groceries, he found his wallet with all its contents and his mobile phone in amongst the mushrooms.

Harper never heard or saw the man who so nearly shot him again and he and Audrey got married the following summer. The Bernards acted as official witnesses. Audrey gained a promotion in the news department and Harper gave up writing his novel, as it seemed rather tame. He got occasional work consulting for his former employers and took a substantial chunk of his inheritance and invested it in Lisa's bookshop as a partner. Lisa and Inez wanted to go and spend a year travelling in Mexico so Harper looked after the cats and ran the shop while they were away, and would sit there behind the desk, the new local oracle for expats, fresh off the Eurostar, who might be feeling a little lost and in need of a kind word and hot cup of tea.

***

About ten months after installing himself behind the cramped wooden desk of the Coin Anglais bookshop, Harper was browsing through various book catalogues online when his mobile buzzed: a text message. *Probably another promotional offer*, he thought. He must receive a dozen a week.

It read: 'Monsieur. You are a man of great discretion and outstanding qualities and courage as you have shown us. If you are interested in a special and highly profitable venture, please meet my associate on the Pont Neuf at six this evening. I am sure you will recognise him. There is no obligation and this invitation will not be extended again'.

The bell above the door rang as another customer stepped inside. Harper looked around the shop, thought about Audrey, thought about how far he had come and about what he wanted from life. Then he moved his thumb across the keypad on his phone and pressed a button.

'Are you sure you want to delete this message?' appeared on the screen.

One more keystroke, 'ok', and it was done. Harper looked up at a slightly lost-looking backpacker.

"Yes, Miss, can I help?"

TRIO

Charlotte's Brooch

For the last three years, Charlotte had been coming to see 'her' cameo brooch nestling serenely in its midnight blue velvet-lined case. The case was on the bottom shelf of the display window of the tiny Polish-owned boutique in the Gallerie Valoi at the Palais Royal. It wasn't the most precious, or even the most beautiful brooch in the window of Kuzemko's, but every Thursday afternoon, for the last three years, Charlotte had stood outside in the covered aisle lined with stone columns, and gazed at the dun oval with its ivory-white bas-relief profile of an unknown eighteenth-century lady. The secret, small thrill of finding the brooch still there week in, week out was a delicious, tiny pleasure. They had made an unspoken bargain, Charlotte and the brooch; as long as Charlotte appeared every Thursday, then the brooch would not allow itself to be sold. And so, for three years, they faithfully kept their silent tryst.

If the lady on the brooch could give you her impression at these moments, she would tell you that Charlotte's heart-shaped face, framed by soft, red curls, was serene. She would say that her pale skin was smooth and her brown eyes shone with the sort of inner light that only those who have suffered on account of their intelligence and free spirit, trapped within this most ordinary of worlds, possess. She would add that her slightly too sensuous lips, kissed with the palest touch of rose lipstick, were pressed lightly together with the merest hint of a smile dancing at the very furthest corners of her mouth. She would conclude that Charlotte was beautiful.

Every Thursday afternoon for three years, Charlotte would tarry in front of the window of Kuzemko's, lost in her reveries. After five minutes she would close her eyes for a few seconds, sigh a sigh that seemed wistful yet content, then she would look briefly at the other pieces in the window, paying her respects lest they should feel jealous at her attention to the brooch. Then she would turn and walk away back to the other world.

But today was different. Today, instead of walking away, Charlotte went to the door of the shop. Her gloved hand lightly held the long brass handle – she paused an instant, then pushed. The little bell tinkled its silvery welcome as the door swung open and Charlotte stepped inside.

Josephine's Cat

Josephine had a cat: a large, lazy ginger-tom. She met him one day on the steps of the back door of her apartment building, picking through the shredded remains of a rubbish bag that had been put beside the overflowing green wheelie-bins. The cat was filthy, skinny and had half of one ear torn away. He looked the sort of cat that would be so self-reliant and mistrustful of people that any friendly human approach or kind word would be greeted by a feline look of contempt, a hiss and a swift escape over the wall. But Josephine's overly big heart melted and she sat on her haunches, some yards from the animal, and clutching her knees, she just stayed there, silent and immobile. Presently, the alley ruffian looked at her, stretched indifferently and strolled diffidently over to her. Still, she did not move or utter a word. Finally, the orange cat stopped just a few inches in front of her. He stretched again and Josephine would later swear that he appeared to shrug as if to say, "Oh well. If this fool wants to love and take care of me, who am I to disappoint her." Then he jumped nimbly onto her lap and allowed himself to be swept up in her arms, cooed at, kissed, hugged and later, fed, cleaned and even endured a visit to the vet for shots and the imposition of a hideous green flea-collar complete with silver bell, and took up principal residence on the kitchen windowsill of Josephine's cosy two-room flat.

"Well, we better give you a name, cat," said Josephine one evening a couple of weeks later. She was sitting on her bed, legs tucked underneath her, tapping out a few paragraphs of her thesis. The cat, already significantly sleeker and glossier than a fortnight previously, jumped onto the bed and rubbed himself sensuously and self-indulgently against his flatmate.

"Hmmm. How about Tobias? No? Monty? No, not Monty. Rusty? Doesn't grab you, eh? OK well, *you* choose. When you have, just let me know." Josephine went back to her typing. The cat, curious at the darting movements of Josephine's slender fingers over the keys, went to investigate and sitting between her hands, he watched the busy fingers tapping away. Deciding that this was a good game, he stretched forward a paw and slapped the keyboard a few times. Josephine stopped typing and watched the screen. One by one, the characters k-o-o-j-2 appeared. The cat withdrew his paw and turned his head to look at Josephine.

"Kooj2? That's the name you want?" The cat, responding to the soft, rich tones of her voice, walked up to her face, which was now resting on her palms, her elbows on the bed.

He gave her a small butt on her upturned nose as if to say, "It's not the name I want, silly girl, it *is* my name."

"Well, Kooj2, time for some milk."

And that was it. Josephine and Kooj2 wandered into the kitchen to see about the milk.

Samuel's Balcony

Samuel stood on his balcony and looked out at the city going about its business below him. Grasping the cool, green-painted metal rail to steady a slight twinge of drunkenness and vertigo, he said aloud, in a voice that could have been all at once, disbelieving, wondrous, rueful and oddly, nervously optimistic, "Bloody hell, I did it! I am actually in bloody Paris!"

The opened French windows leading to the kitchen of the sixth-floor apartment on the Rue Rivoli and half-emptied bottle of Bordeaux on the beech wood table within accounted for his presence on the balcony and also for his mild unsteadiness. However, how Samuel came to find himself in Paris was a rather more complicated story.

The bare bones of Samuel's situation would be too corpulent and unwieldy to recount if fully fleshed. Suffice to say that he was thirty-four34 years old and recently, but almost painlessly, ditched and divorced by his independently very wealthy (at least, "Daddy" was wealthy which was almost the same thing), artist wife of nine years, who had abandoned him to take up with a twenty-five-year-old lute-player and folk-singer called Barry, who wore a caftan, lived in a gypsy caravan in Solihull and had an almost deviant interest in Prokoviev and the writings of John Donne. Having only had a couple of brief student couplings at university before meeting and marrying Diana (whom he had wooed away from a rather frightening lesbian called Brenda who had a penchant for strawberry ice-cream, Ancient Greek and S&M, often in combination), Samuel felt more like an awkward teenager with women rather than the successful, good-looking-in-a-careless-way, gentle, humorous advertising copywriter that he was. He found himself freshly divorced and alone in a picture-postcard cottage in Buckinghamshire with no real friends and a vague feeling that he had missed out on something; that somewhere, just out of his earshot and vision, the world was having fun.

He took two weeks off work, sat down in the kitchen of the cottage with an iron kettle on the Aga; an old, brown and seemingly bottomless teapot which was missing the lid, ever since Diana had launched it at him for suffocating her muse (which meant that he had been somewhat less than enthusiastic at the suggestion of letting her roll around with Barry in front of him); the phone numbers of all the takeaways in a ten-mile radius that would deliver to this tiny hamlet; and a case of good, red Burgundy. He set to work writing out all the things he liked and wanted to do and all the things he disliked and didn't want to do. He scarcely thought about his ex-wife, let alone pine for her. As far as he was concerned, Diana and Barry could bounce around the caravan quoting John Donne to each other until doomsday and, "Good luck to them both," he toasted, polishing off another glass of Pommard which went surprisingly well with lamb rogan josh and garlic naan.

His list took several editions to perfect, and the stone-flagged kitchen floor was strewn with crumpled A4 sheets, paper aeroplanes, fans and other unlikely origami. However, on day eight of this slightly inebriated, tea-curry-pizza-crispy-aromatic-duck fuelled exile in his chocolate-box hermitage, Samuel leant back in the unvarnished oak chair and holding one hand on the back of his neck kneading the knots, he held the completed, definitive 'Declaration of M'Independence', as he had christened it, aloft in triumph. Three months later he was at Waterloo station about to board the Eurostar to take him to Paris and a new life. A better life. His own life.

The Confluence of Events

At precisely three-fifteen, just as Charlotte stepped lightly onto the flagstones outside the shop with a thrill in her heart as clear and musical as the bell of the shop door, Josephine came rushing down the stairs of her apartment building and flew out into the street narrowly avoiding a collision with a postman's trolley and a very startled elderly gentleman, sporting a silver moustache that a retired musketeer would have been proud of.

Issuing apologies in French and English, Josephine left the old soldier staring after her, half vexed at nearly being knocked off his feet and half intoxicated with the imperceptibly scented air left by Josephine's perfume and the rapidly retreating shape of her silhouette.

"Ravissante," was all he could muster and fell to reverie of beauties past, conquered and unconquered.

As usual, Josephine was late. She had a tutorial with her supervisor and Dr. Villon did not like to be kept waiting; his ire was always manifested by arch sarcasm and much tutting. His study, where he held his tutorials, was an attic in the Rue Saint Honoré; it always smelled of cats, stale cigarettes and some cheap musky male eau de toilette, although Josephine had never seen a cat, saw him smoke or caught the faintest whiff of this cologne from Dr. Villon when he was reading over her shoulder as she struggled with some obscure Mediaeval text.

She half sprinted into the Palais Royal quadrant at the very moment that Charlotte was walking in the opposite direction, her hand clutching on tightly to the little velvet box, which did not contain the brooch, much to the lady on the brooch's chagrin, but rather a simple gold and onyx antique ring. She knew Patrick would love it and as it was a time for changes and to break with everything that had been expected of her all her life, she was going to offer it to him when she proposed that evening.

Getting up from one of the green-painted iron benches in the garden of the Palais and stretching contentedly and exaggeratedly, Samuel stuck his pencil behind his ear in a somewhat pretentious way then thought better of it and put it in his shirt pocket and gathered up his sketchpad, and was about to wander off in search of a glass of wine. As he looked behind him for a final check that he had left nothing behind, he saw a swirl of blonde hair and a multi--coloured scarf with a vaguely oriental design dancing like the tattered banner of a charging Carolingian knight in the slipstream of a young woman dashing headlong along the covered walkway, and definitely not in the restrained rather, un-exuberant Parisian fashion. Fascinated, Samuel did not notice the red-headed woman rather dreamily ambling in the opposite direction. Then he saw her. Then he saw what was about to happen. Before he could react, the lithe power of running graduate student collided full on with the love-struck Midwest rebel and both women collapsed in an undignified but, in Samuel's eyes, very attractive heap.

Ever the gentleman and hero of his own unwritten novel, Samuel rushed over to the stunned pair and offered both hands, extended in succour. He felt the smallest of pulls on one hand as the younger woman leapt up as if on springs and the slightly, but only slightly, heavier tug on the other hand as the more mature woman arose a little more cautiously.

Then horror!

"My ring! Where is it?" the dismay and distress was as if of a mother for a missing child, "It was in a little blue velvet box, I must have dropped it." And she began a feverish search with panicked eyes that saw nothing.

Within a few seconds all three were ravenously scanning the grass, the path and the shop doorways in the immediate vicinity. Josephine had forgotten all about her tutorial and Samuel was for the moment, in his head, Sir Galahad seeking the Holy Grail.

They spotted it at the same moment, cunningly hidden under a large amber and yellow leaf. Josephine and Samuel lunged at precisely the same instant and the clash of heads was inevitable and the sound, impressive. Giving a little gasp of alarm, Charlotte, the ring forgotten for just that second, rushed over to give what assistance she could. But she stopped short. Samuel and Josephine both rose a little gingerly from the collision, both with one hand on their respective foreheads nursing a rapidly forming lump and both with the other hand holding the little blue box.

No one spoke.

There was a pause and both hands offered the box to Charlotte but seemed reluctant to let go of each other.

Stepping close, Charlotte gently prised the box form the two hands and joined them back together.

"There," she said, "that's better."

Charlotte didn't tarry to thank the couple as they didn't seem aware of her, the Palais Royal or anything else in the world except each other.

With a half-smile and a sigh only reserved for those in the deepest state of contentment, Charlotte left the new acquaintances and walked slowly out of the gates and onto the Rue Saint Honoré.

THE WEDDING PRESENT

Wilfredo Hernandez was a happy man. He was far from rich, he had never had much money but he was proud that he had always provided for his family; that his two surviving children had shoes, books and pencils for school growing up; and that his wife, Delia, only scolded him in jest.

And now, in Wilfredo's sixtieth year, his oldest child, Ernesto, an electrician in the new resort that had sprung up from the sands by the Pacific, was happily married with three healthy boys of his own, and his little Rosita, his youngest child (a gift to him and Delia after the tragic loss of her older brother, Carlos, at the age of 8 from meningitis), born eighteen years before, was getting married.

She is a good girl, thought Wilfredo as he rode the ancient former American school bus. It was now painted in gay colours with the words 'Jesus El Salvador' emblazoned on the sides, and a photograph of a topless Aida Yespica, the Venezuelan supermodel, torn from a magazine on the dashboard alongside a small plastic statue of the Virgin Mary, *She will make a good wife.*

It was true. Rosa, raven-haired, dark-eyed and only a trifle plump, he felt, had a joy for life, a lively mind and was hard-working, bringing in much needed cash to the household by working diligently as a cleaner for several American retired couples living in the same resort where her brother plied his trade. She was an excellent cook, thanks to her mother, made a lot of her own clothes, and had a beautiful singing voice... and she was in love and about to be married to Jorge.

And this is why Wilfredo was so proud. Jorge Diaz was 24, spoke English and had been to Miami to train as a chef and was now the sous chef at the new restaurant, Las Olas, conveniently located just at the gates of the resort, so tritely named, El Dorado ("The gringos love it," so claimed the oleaginous PR director for the resort, Miguel, who made everyone call him Mike and whose bonhomie was as phoney as his toupée).

Yes, Wilfredo's musings continued over the din of the engine as he bumped and bounced in his seat, half holding onto his appropriately battered straw hat as the warm wind rushed into the open windows ("Latino AirCon," as Ernesto called it). *Yes, Jorge is going places. He is a good man and will be a good father and he will have his own restaurant someday. Rosita is a lucky girl... and Jorge is a lucky boy!*

So lost in these happy, idle thoughts, Wilfredo half forgot where he was and what he was doing. A blare from the bus klaxon and the squeal of hot brakes brought him sharply back to the present moment and just in time... *"Dios!* My stop!"

The door would have opened had there been one, and Wilfredo stepped down, not onto the dusty path that lined the roads in his village some fifteen miles away, but onto fresh tarmac, the still slightly tacky, oil-slick, wet-look asphalt of the brand new shopping mall in San Lorenzo.

***

Tom Wyche was a rarity in San Lorenzo; he didn't live at El Dorado, he didn't play golf, and he did speak Spanish. An oddity among the mainly monolingual expats who had come in droves to retire to the sun at a third of the cost of doing the same thing in Arizona, Tom was sixty-two, originally from Maryland and spoke Spanish thanks to the fact his father trained a few horses near Fair Hill, where all of the grooms and stall cleaners were Mexican, and as a boy hanging around the barns all summer while his father was busy with training, Tom, a quick learner, had picked up a range of skills from riding restless two-year-old colts to driving a tractor, from fixing broken doors and windows to speaking reasonably good, if rather earthy, Spanish.

The army, college, career as the owner of a small construction firm, marriage, kids and divorce had all followed in the typical order of things and as soon as the crash of 2008 seemed inevitable, Tom sold his business, his house and his Ford F250, and having been assiduous in preparing all his documents, with the assistance of a superb, if bossy, immigration lawyer, he left the US forever.

His ex-wife, Gloria, who had long ago remarried and lived in Vancouver with her architect husband, told him to take care and wished him well. His twin sons, Tom Jr and Tim had left several years before. Tom Jr was doing something financial in Singapore and Tim was bumming around Europe, teaching English, smoking pot and chasing girls (usually with not inconsiderable success). Tom had nothing keeping him and he decided he wanted to be in Latin America and build things again. But not buildings this time. Thirty years of building houses was enough. So now, he intended to turn his hobby into a full time job. Tom had come to build boats; traditional, old-fashioned wooden boats.

Thankfully, he didn't need to earn any money from it, but that would be nice too, he thought. He did it for the joy of the craft. He had owned a sixteen-foot wooden Dory fishing boat on the Chesapeake and, spurning fibreglass and chrome, he copied the design and built one of his own. It took him three years but it was beautiful and when his neighbour offered him six thousand dollars for it, Tom was inspired.

So, he bought an old truck and two derelict fishing shacks on the coast a few miles along from San Lorenzo and did them up himself, installing electricity, plumbing and ceiling fans (he hated air conditioning), and with his personable nature and decent Spanish, he achieved in turning these tumbledown hovels into a small but perfectly comfortable home for himself and a well-equipped workshop for his boat-building. He seldom wore a shirt or shoes and his skin was deeply tanned, so much so that his tattoos recklessly and drunkenly acquired while in the army in Germany, were barely visible. His hair, thick and white, was clean but wild and unruly, and he was always bareheaded. His hands were strong and slender but bore the scars of many years of working in his craft. Old army discipline meant that despite his rather unconventional lifestyle, he cleaned his own house, ironed his own clothes and was always close shaved. He had a local widow woman, Mabel, come in twice a week to cook for him as he was useless in the kitchen. She would give him a list of food to buy and she would cook up several dishes, which he would keep in the noisy fridge that was always working overtime in the intense heat. The fact that after a couple of years she occasionally stayed overnight seemed to suit them both and generally they watched TV, ate a little dinner, drank a little wine and just lay in the dark holding one another, listening to the 'tchak tchak' of the geckos and the sea breeze ruffling through the palms. The only thing Tom did cook was the odd fish he caught himself when taking out one of his boats for a test run. Thus he had lived for nearly eight years now and had seen San Lorenzo grow from a small town with nothing but palm trees and plantains, a single store called the San Jose Mini Super and a reputation for good fishing, to a thriving town with bright white towering condos for retired middle Americans, two golf courses, gourmet restaurants, multi-screen sports bars, fast food outlets and stores that the locals could only dream of shopping in. Tom generally spurned the fancy restaurants, avoided the golf course like the plague and kept out of the gringo bars, preferring to sip the odd rum and coke at the little Mini Super which had half-heartedly set out a couple of plastic tables and a few mismatched chairs under a corrugated iron canopy, thus doubling as a bar laughingly known as Las Terrazas. Still, the booze was cheap and they did great breaded chicken fingers and a diabolically hot sauce for two bucks.

Why he chose San Lorenzo when he did can only be put down to the same instinct that compelled him to sell up just before the credit crunch bit: a sort of prescience for change. In any event, he arrived when there was virtually nothing and now that the influx of gringos with spare cash and nothing but time had arrived, he had orders for boats to last him the next three years. He always asked for half the money up front. After all, some of these retired types were getting on a bit. But if the inevitable happened before the boat was built, Tom returned the deposit minus cost of materials to the widow.

And it was this full order book that impelled him into San Lorenzo today. He needed a few things from the hardware store. Most of the time he got his wood and other materials from local traders and farmers from the interior but occasionally when he needed nails or a new blade for a plane, he would get in his formally red, now sun bleached pink truck and drive the six miles into town. No longer along a bumpy rutted dusty track that was nigh on impassable in rainy season when it was transformed into an oozing serpent of mud, but a shiny new four-lane highway connecting the whole country from the northern frontier to the southern border via the fleshpots of the rapidly growing capital.

Tom pulled into the vast parking lot, full of old American and newer Japanese SUVs with the occasional German all-terrain vehicle, several yellow, rusting, dented but highly polished taxis and a bright silver Hummer, belonging to the local servant of the people, the town mayor Rafael Avila, who had, by stroke of luck, found himself the sole owner of the choicest ocean-front lots when the town council 'voted' to privatise the land. The Mayor, in case you are wondering, was coincidentally the brother of 'Mike' Miguel, the PR guru of El Dorado. Again, by sheer happenstance, the Mayor's other brother, Juan, owned the main condo construction company in San Lorenzo and his sister, Margarita, ran the leading estate agents. The locals, who never seemed bitter because most of them depended on the Mayor's family for their livelihoods, often called San Lorenzo, *Ciudad Avila*. However, the Avilas were invested in the town. The family had grown melons there since long before independence and they were proud of growing a gleaming, modern town out of the sand and dust. True, the locals could only dream of eating in the town's fancy French and Italian restaurants but on birthdays and saints days, they could stretch to the local McDonalds where an enterprising manager had recently installed a karaoke system and created the McWedding reception; it was not an uncommon sight to see the blushing bride tucking into a quarter-pounder while her proud and slightly tipsy father sang along with Julio Iglesias. They even provided mini wedding cake brownies with frosting and a blind eye was turned if the guests wanted to provide their own liquid refreshments.

There was a small but decently equipped public health clinic and a good school built and sponsored by the Avila family, and since drink-driving and speeding laws were seldom enforced, and the Avilas were also patrons of the week-long festival of flowers every April, when the entire town got drunk on the local rum and Cerveza Nacional, stopped work and spent every night delighting in the fireworks handed out for free (of which most Latin Americans are so inordinately fond), no one really begrudged them their millions.

Wilfedo had spent his entire life in his village of Santa Maria. He considered himself fortunate; the civil war, the death squads, the terror had largely bypassed Santa Maria. It was not strategically situated and was most often ignored by rebels and government troops alike save for the occasional visit to steal the odd rusting car or round up a few scrawny chickens. Neither side had any use for watermelons, so the Avilas and the equally insignificant village of San Lorenzo were largely left alone. Wilfredo was proud that he could read and write thanks to an Italian Jesuit, Father Pierro, who taught him and a few of the other boys who weren't needed in the fields under an old Ceiba tree, and although he had never been to the capital, he read all the newspapers that occasionally found their way into the village, often months old, but earning him the reputation as the local scholar. As it happened, the only other diligent student spelling out words from the bible and the lives of the saints under that Ceiba tree was our old friend, Rafa Avila. He did leave for the capital as soon as he turned fifteen and well, we know how he turned out.

Wilfredo went into the family business, fishing. They had two boats. One little more than a raft for close-to-shore catches and the other a twelve-foot kayak which although sitting in it redefined the phrase, *for those in peril on the sea*, never capsized and helped Wilfredo, his mother (his father having succumbed to pneumonia when he was ten) and his seven brothers and sisters survive and get married.

Now that Rosita and Ernesto were earning, and Delia had a small stand which was famous along twenty miles of the coast for the delicious breaded red snapper it served, Wilfredo was able to fish just three days a week. He had a heart murmur that had been diagnosed by the visiting doctor (another social amenity sponsored by the Avilas) and was advised to take things easier, which he found frustrating.

So, when the joyous news of Rosa's wedding was announced, Wilfredo decided to devote his time to making the lovebirds a wonderful wedding present.

Jorge had an old car and his father had left him a small adobe house on the edge of Santa Maria. But the house was old and in need of repair. So Wilfredo decided that his wedding present would be to build a new bathroom and kitchen for his daughter and new son. Like all the men in the village, Wilfredo grew up learning how to mend nets, repair the boats and most families built their own houses. Now, although the houses were built in the old style, electricity, running water and sanitation were the norm along with incongruous satellite-TV dishes. Jorge's house did have electricity and running water but the bathroom was old and dingy, and the kitchen was not fit for a chef and his excellent cook of a bride. Having discussed plans with Jorge and keeping it secret from Rosa, Wilfredo had begun the process and the rooms were freshly plastered and painted, and Ernesto had put in lights and had managed to get a modest but attractive bathroom suite from a condo that was being 'updated' by its new, rather fussy Bostonian owners who were happy to let him have it for nothing since he offered to take it away and rewire their apartment for free. The kitchen had proved more of a problem. Space was limited and although the oven and the fridge had been found and were ready for installation and Jorge was delighted with everything, there remained one final item to find and fit. Ironically enough, it was the kitchen sink. Wilfredo regarded this as his solemn undertaking and he had heard of a new store in San Lorenzo that had every type of tap and sink you could buy, some even made in

China. And as he stood on the baking tarmac listening to the whoosh of enormous cars with blackened windows speed by behind him, he looked up and saw the huge yellow letters, ten feet tall on the roof of the building scream the name 'Daly', he felt the thrill of the explorer well up within him. He took off his hat, awestruck as if standing in the Vatican itself, and walked slowly towards the gleaming new hyperstore.

Rafa Avila was having a bad week. Normally good natured and affable with a generosity of spirit enabled by extreme wealth and love of life, today was not going to plan. He had terrible heartburn and sitting in the cockpit of his Hummer, despite the icy cold air conditioning, sweating in his Egyptian cotton shirt and light grey Italian suit; he removed his black-rimmed rectangular French glasses and pinched his nose. Corpulent but not fat, bald and moustached, Rafael Avila usually cut a debonair, sophisticated figure. Today, however, he felt jaded and bile-ridden. Vexed with his wife, Susana, who had texted him from Miami to say she was staying on an extra week to 'pick up a few things', Rafa grudgingly admitted to himself how much he missed her. Married for thirty years with four fantastic kids, all graduates or studying in the US, Rafa was not the slightest bit bothered at his wife's shopping spree but he missed her. He missed her sense of humour, her wisdom and even at fifty-five he missed her warm, voluptuous body in his bed at night. Rafael had been something of a lothario at the university in the capital, where he had studied law until the civil war had interfered with his studies...that is to say, they had dragged his professor from his bed one night and shot him in the car park of the national soccer stadium. And when he fled to America with the help of the professor's widow, who was born in Texas, and enrolled at college in Amarillo, his Latin-lover looks and brooding manner had gained him many conquests. Yet since the day he met Susana, shortly after returning home armed with a law degree and full of lofty ideas of modernising his country, he had been what his brother, that idiot, the lubricious Miguel had called 'untypically and pitifully faithful'. She had been gone a month. "Everything you can get in Miami you can buy in the Royal Mall for not much more," Rafael said ruefully to himself. "And now this! Begging at the door of a Mexican! Unthinkable!"

Rafael Avila was rich. And he had become rich through manipulation, force of character and some extremely creative bookkeeping. He had almost single-handedly built San Lorenzo from nothing and although he glossed over some of the less than scrupulous methods he had employed to get where he was today, he was proud of his town, proud of the jobs it provided and proud of the fact that he could walk (or rather drive) down the street and receive what seemed to him genuine waves and smiles from the locals. In fact, unlike his oafish brother who was a slave to the gringo retirees or his avaricious sister, Rafael loved San Lorenzo. His life was different now and he spent his days in endless meetings and at pompous society events, glad-handing the local dignitaries or politicians visiting from the capital, or schmoozing investors on the golf course. Golf! What a ridiculous game! He loathed it with an almost unreasonable passion. It gave him blisters on his hands, pains in the arches of his feet and sand in his teeth, but from years of socialising he had actually become a reasonable player; that is to say, just good enough to lose when it was expedient to do so. He lived in suits. He hated suits. And although he wore them with the easy grace of one accustomed to bespoke tailoring, Rafa was never happier than when he and Susana put on jeans and cowboy boots and went off to their ranch thirty miles inland, going on long trail rides and taking a picnic of cold chicken and the deliciously sweet, juicy watermelons which had sustained his family for generations.

And here he sat, drenched and bilious and gripping the steering wheel, he steeled himself, took a deep breath and opened the door. He was here at the brand new Daly superstore with 'everything to make your house a home' to meet the new regional director, Brandon Suarez from Mexico City. *What kind of name is Brandon for a Latino?* Rafa asked himself through gritted teeth. Daly Group had invested heavily in a huge home-improvement store, and with so many retired wealthy folk in the area, business was good. The store employed over 100 people and was an asset to San Lorenzo but apart from the jobs, there had not been the same commitment in the town as other outsiders had brought. The KFC and McDonalds sponsored the children's unit at the health clinic. Sears had paid for all the school books, and the supermarkets, banks and upmarket chain stores had all contributed to the social wellbeing of the town.

Daly had done nothing despite several letters from the Mayor. So the Mayor had come in person to meet with Sr Suarez who was visiting San Lorenzo as part of a tour of his region. The objective for Rafael was modest. He was seeking sponsorship for the local youth soccer league; some kit, maybe a minibus, a few thousand to have the Daly name embroidered on shirts and painted on a bus and lots of goodwill and free advertising in return. Everyone played the game. Mutual back-scratching made the world go round. But this Brandon, instead of falling over himself to cooperate suggested a meeting at the store to discuss the matter. *To discuss the matter! At his store! Who the hell does he think he is?* Rafael's heartburn flared again and instead of going into Daly, he stopped off at the little pharmacy in the mall to buy some Maalox. His spirits were lifted a little at the warm reception he received from the staff and one young mother even presented her baby for him to bestow a kiss on her forehead. Puffing out his chest and drawing in his Armani belt a notch, Rafael Avila took a swig from the bottle of chalky antacid and marched purposefully toward the sliding glass electric doors of the Daly superstore.

Tom Wyche seldom hurried. From his space in the parking lot to the door of Daly was less than thirty yards but that could often take Tom ten minutes. He would say

hello and exchange a few words with the omnipresent
security guards stationed outside just about every store in
town. Each armed with baton, cuffs and a superannuated
Taurus 38 revolver, which had never been, nor, God forbid,
ever would be fired. He stopped to say hello to friends and
acquaintances effortlessly slipping between Spanish and
English depending on the need and he paused to watch
the old, almost psychedelically painted ex-American school
bus pull noisily out of the parking lot, belching thick
black smoke from its broken exhaust. Waving to Angelo,
the young security guard who was leaning on the wall by
the door of Daly trying to look cool and failing, cracking a
huge boyish grin as he chatted with Maria, one of the till
girls on her break who giggled at his antics, Tom, dressed
oppressively for him in a white cotton short-sleeved shirt,
blue shorts and a pair of green deck shoes that invariably
gave him blisters, walked from the searing heat of the
parking lot and through the automatic sliding doors into
the freezer-cold of the highly air-conditioned megastore.

Wilfredo walked a little hesitantly through the open
doors into the vast warehouse and he might as well have
been walking onto the surface of an alien planet. To begin
with, it was freezing cold and the loud hum of the air
conditioners reminded him of the sound of bombers in
the old war films he liked to watch on his ancient black
and white TV set. Delia had teased him about that as she
had a colour portable in the kitchen to watch her 'novelas'
but Wilfredo said he only liked old films and they were
always in black and white anyway.

Gazing around the two-storey mammoth of a building with shelves stacked twenty feet high on both levels with gadgets and tools, paints and all manner of items that seemed very unfamiliar to him, Wilfredo could see no taps or sinks or anything remotely resembling what he had come to find. From somewhere above the din of the air conditioners, he was aware that some indistinguishable pop music was playing, interrupted every now and then by the enthusiastic, almost frenetic voice of someone urging him to buy Sherwin Williams white emulsion at 'two for one, only at Daly'! He already felt like a foreigner in his own country and standing in the middle of the ground floor, his hat still in his hands, he looked around and felt even more of out of place. The store was populated by black and yellow uniformed staff with broad smiles and nametags with Anglicised versions of their names. Pablo had become Paul, Ricardo was now Richard and Consuelo, was just Connie. But stranger than the staff were the customers. *Almost all Americans,* Wilfredo supposed, he hadn't seen that many in real life. The new highway had bypassed Santa Maria and very few visitors made it to the village as there was not much of interest for them; no curio stores nor ancient ruins, and only the locals knew about Delia's red snapper. He looked at them. He stared. He couldn't help it. All the men, mostly over sixty, looked so tall, so healthy. They seemed to be wearing some sort of uniform too; pastel short-sleeved shirts, expensive-looking gold watches, white linen trousers or white or khaki shorts, white socks and leather sandals. Wilfredo thought the men looked handsome, most of them with paunches spilling magnificently over their leather belts. A paunch was a sign of prosperity and highly regarded in Santa Maria. The few women all seemed to have golden-grey hair peeping out from large straw hats and were too skinny for Wilfredo's taste. "A woman should have the figure of a guitar," his oldest brother, Manuel, used to say.

"Or a bottle of Coca-Cola!" chipped in his younger brother, Rodrigo.

Wilfredo felt very uncomfortable. He shivered slightly and nervously approached 'Paul'. Half afraid the young man wouldn't speak Spanish, Wilfredo asked slowly and clearly whether the store sold kitchen sinks. "Of course, Caballero. Upstairs, first floor at the back," and with a vague wave of his hand indicating the heavens and a winning smile, Paul was gone.

But there were no stairs! Suddenly and to his horror, Wilfredo saw a tall man with a shock of thick white hair seemingly ascending to heaven without walking! Wilfredo crossed himself and checked to see whether anyone else had witnessed this miracle. Then another man, then another, then a couple, all seemed to be levitating. Now, Wilfredo was not a stupid man but he had little experience or use for the modern world. He hadn't even been in San Lorenzo for fifteen years so superstores resembling ice-cold caverns and now flying people were all a little overwhelming. But not being a stupid man, Wilfredo also reasoned that these ascending souls were not angels but that there must be some sort of moving staircase to the upper floor. He walked round a display of immense barbecue sets and arrived at the bottom of the escalator. And he froze.

About the same moment that Wilfredo stood rooted to the spot at the foot of the escalator while a couple of people squeezed past him to climb aboard, one of whom, a sharp-featured, sharp-elbowed woman, tutted audibly, Rafael Avila emerged from the store manager's office after the briefest of meetings with Sr Brandon Suarez. Rafa was wearing a very self-satisfied and not-too-discreet grin on his face and his heartburn had disappeared. The meeting with the Mexican had gone well. Rafael had lied his head off but got what he wanted. He explained that he was delighted to welcome such an important and distinguished businessman to San Lorenzo but was terribly sorry that he could not tarry as he had a meeting with the representatives of a large… (and here he hesitated. For the life of him he couldn't remember which country the main competitors to Daly came from. He knew it was one of the Nordic ones, full of snow and tall blondes with great teeth. He had read about their management techniques in Forbes) … err, Scandinavian company who had just applied for a permit to build a store by the highway. Suddenly, the haughty Sr Suarez crumbled. "Well, of course, Sr Mayor, I know you are busy but I am delighted to say that Daly will be honoured to accommodate any proposal you have for

youth football sponsorship... in full." The 'in full' was
so pregnant with meaning it practically gave birth in the
room, Rafael would later say.

As Suarez hurried to open the door for the Mayor,
Rafael Avila paused and turned, and with the meerest
twinkle in his eye asked, "You don't happen to play golf
do you, Sr Brandon?"

Now, a few moments later and still congratulating
himself on his cunning victory, Rafael was just about to
step onto the down escalator but stopped mid-stride and
reversed a pace to watch the most extraordinary scene
unfolding down below.

Dressed in a white shirt buttoned up to the collar,
faded jeans. Sunday-best black shoes and clutching a
battered straw hat stood a short, slender old man with
short black hair, flecked with grey. His skin was dark-
tanned, deeply lined and leathery from years out in the
sun. He was chattering and laughing nervously and
was flanked by Paul and Connie in their smart Daly
uniforms, each gripping an elbow gently encouraging the
reluctant man to step forward onto the escalator while
bemused shoppers edged round the trio and continued
their upward journey. The old man was blushing in
embarrassment although you couldn't tell from his dark
sunburnt skin. Wilfredo knew now what the escalator
was but never having seen one in his life, let alone been
on one, he was ashamed to say he was scared to take that
first step and the gentle cajoling of the well-meaning
staff was just making him more flustered.

Rafael Avila was about to call out some words of encouragement when a tall, white-haired man tore past him and sprinted down the steps of the down escalator shouting for the trio planted at the bottom of the up escalator to wait. Rafael, driven by an unknown impulse and in a manner not at all in keeping with his lofty and dignified position as mayor of San Lorenzo and, panting slightly, followed close behind at a slightly less rapid lick.

Rafa recognised the white-haired man. That American boat builder who lived just out of town, Bob was it, or Tom, something monosyllabic. All Americans seemed to have just one syllable names. But this one was a decent sort. He spoke Spanish and every year at the Christmas fiesta at the town hall he discreetly handed Rafael two generous cheques; one for the school and another for the animal welfare programme started by Susana. It was a distinguished fact that there were no stray dogs in San Lorenzo. A programme of neutering and a slightly chaotic but large sanctuary was another thing to be proud of.

The two staff had now stepped back from the old man's side and he was engaged in an animated conversation with the tall American who was offering him his arm as you would to a blind man to cross a busy road. Feeling sheepish but clutching the arm offered to him, Wilfredo was about to take the plunge onto the moving bottom step but his nerve failed him at the last moment. Tom just stood by his side patiently and continued talking to him gently.

"Wilfredito! Is that you?" It had been almost forty years since he last saw him, but Rafael Avila recognised his former classmate from the Ceiba tree. "Wilfredo Hernandez! It's me, Rafa Avila!"

This was almost too much for Wilfredo and he gasped and in his open-mouthed shock didn't notice Tom gently walk him onto the escalator. As the two men, one tall, one short slowly began to ascend, Wilfredo dropped his hat and it bounced gently down to the bottom of the escalator. Seizing the hat before it had ceased rolling, the Mayor bounded up the escalator after the most recent passengers and all three stumbled off the top at the same time.

With a nod to Tom whose arm was still solidly in the clutch of his recent travelling companion, Rafael Avila brushed off the battered straw hat and without pausing for breath began to talk nineteen to the dozen to his childhood friend. Wilfredo could not get a word in edgeways which was just as well as he was dumbstruck by the events of the last few minutes. As Rafa handed back the hat to the astonished old man, Wilfredo reached out for it in an almost trance-like state and was aware that Rafael had paused for breath and seemed to be waiting for some sort of response. Tom, correctly judging the man's confusion took the opportunity to gently prize his arm from the nervous grasp of Wilfredo and buying him a few seconds to collect himself warmly greeted the Mayor and asked how Sra Avila was. Before Rafael could answer, Wilfredo came to his senses and not only recognising the bald, chubby but immaculately dressed man before him suddenly remembered that this man was the mayor of San Lorenzo and the richest man in the province... "Rafael! Err... Sr Mayor. I don't kn-know what to say. It is such an honour, Your Honour. My hat, we thank you," Wilfredo was babbling.

"Fredo! It's me, Rafa. How long has it been? How old were we, what fifteen, sixteen? Ah, remember those days? Before the civil war, before the Junta? How's Paco and Lucho? Is Soledad still alive? How's that beautiful girl who was sweet on you, Delia? Tell me everything my friend!" Rafael Avila was punctuating his every word with the most extravagant, sincere and almost alarming handshaking of his stunned companion who held his hat limply in one hand while the other was embraced in the warm clasp of the Mayor.

Of course, Wilfredo knew that the Avilas had made good and that Rafael had been mayor for fifteen years but he never imagined meeting him again or that Rafa Avila would remember him. Even though the two men had spent the bulk of the last sixty years (save the five years that Rafael was at college in the States) living less than fifteen miles apart, the trajectory of their lives might just have well meant they had lived on different continents.

Tom, ever gracious, wanted to make things a bit easier for the old man. "Well, well. Fancy that, so you know Rafa from school, do you Sr?"

"Wilfredo. Wilfredo Hernandez. Yes, from Father Pierro's class. He taught us to read and write."

"But you were better at spelling than I was, Fredo," chuckled the Mayor.

"I'm Tom. *Mucho gusto*."

"Yes, *mucho gusto,* Sr Tom."

The next fifteen minutes were a blur for Wilfredo. The mayor taking him by the arm walked him round and round the upper floor of the store and the two men rode down and up the escalator half a dozen times while lost in their animated reminiscence. Tom, having excused himself and taking no offense at being virtually ignored was on his way down the escalator as the two old friends were on their seventh or eighth trip up. As the three men passed each other, Rafael Avila turned to Tom and said to his rapidly descending back, "Sr Tom, Fredo is a fisherman. He has a wooden boat. You should see it."

Tom smiled and as he stepped off the bottom step just as the other two men stepped off the top step, he gesticulated that he would wait there.

There had been quite a commotion in Daly since the Mayor and an old man had been going up and down the escalators for a good while now and the staff and customers had watched in amused fascination. But things were returning to normal and as the Mayor and Wilfredo came down the escalator for the final time to join Tom, the three men walked out of the frigid air of the store into the blaring midday heat of the parking lot. The acrid smell of cheap petrol, burnt tarmac and exhaust fumes bit deeply into their lungs and shouting to be heard over the traffic, Rafael invited the two men to have coffee at the Town Hall. Wilfredo felt self-conscious and to go to the town hall as the guest of the Mayor was really too much. Tom, again judging the situation perfectly, and with a suspicion that Sr Avila was not a pompous snob, suggested that he would take Wilfredo in his truck and that the Mayor follow him in the Hummer. Rafael agreed. It was noon now and he didn't have the meeting with the chief of Police until three. Besides, the Police Chief was his youngest sister, Esmerelda's, oldest boy, Francisco, so Uncle Rafa might be a bit late without a problem!

Eschewing the Starbucks and the new cocktail bar in town, Tom drove the couple of miles to the familiar corrugated-iron awning of the Terrazas café at the Mini Super and going round to let Wilfredo out of the passenger side because the door always stuck, the two men took a seat at one of the lopsided plastic tables. With a blast of the horn and a cloud of dust, the huge silver Hummer pulled up and the Mayor, now divested of his grey suit jacket and Hermes tie came and joined his companions.

Simon, the owner of the Mini Super and his wife, Teresa, were stunned to see the Mayor perched on an upturned Fanta crate (there was only one chair today. Bloody kids!), flapping his manicured hands to ward off the persistent buzzing of the odd fly and calling for a rum and coke with a slice of lime! However, within an hour or so and after a few glasses and a generous helping of the breaded chicken fingers and the extra hot sauce, it seemed as if the three men had been coming there to meet for years.

"So it's decided then," said Rafael. "I am cancelling my meetings and we are going to see your boat and Delia, and try some of that snapper you have been going on about."

"No, Sr Mayor, err, Rafa, we cannot. Delia isn't expecting company and I am late already."

"Nonsense, my friend! Call her! Here, use my mobile," and Rafael handed Wilfredo his Gresso Regal titanium phone, one of only 333 made and a snip from the Russian company of opulent excess at $4700 bought by Susana, on her last trip to Miami for his birthday. (Tom had a $15 Alcatel).

Wilfredo protested, "I can't do that, Sr Rafael."

"Go ahead, it's just a mobile!"

"But Rafa, we don't have a phone!"

Nevertheless, although the Mayor was a bit drunk, he was the Mayor, so the three men rose, a trifle unsteadily, and made their way to their cars.

"Better come in the truck, Mr Mayor," said Tom. After all, despite the rather lax attitude to drink-driving, it wouldn't do for the Mayor to be caught driving a little the worse for wear.

Nodding deliberately and appreciatively, Rafael agreed and the three men squeezed into the rusting truck and drove the ten miles to Santa Maria.

"Did you get it?" were Delia's first words to Wilfredo. "Did you get the sink?"

"Oh Dios, the sink! Delia, I..."

"You daft old goat! Where have you bee—" Delia stopped in mid-scold. Emerging from the far side of the truck was the grinning face of a friend she hadn't seen in a lifetime.

What followed were hugs and kisses, introductions, more rum, the famed and indeed delicious red snapper; someone produced a guitar, and Jorge and Rosa arrived. People sang, people laughed, people wept a little and Tom, lighting a pipe (which he very seldom did), strolled off with Wilfredo to talk about fishing and look at his boat.

It was evening before the party broke up. Jorge took the Mayor back to his Hummer while Tom inspected Wilfredo's work in the soon to be newlyweds' house. As he left he arranged to pick Wilfredo up the next day so he could complete his wedding present purchase at Daly.

The wedding was four weeks away and Tom spent most of his days in Santa Maria helping Wilfredo finish everything in Jorge's house. A week before the wedding, it was ready, complete with kitchen sink, and both men were very proud of their work. Mabel had joined them some evenings, and she and Delia cooked tasty chicken or fish meals, served on earthenware plates overflowing with yucca and plantains, rice and beans, corn and avocado, and they often chatted about the old days, as older people do, late into the evening.

Rafael Avila popped over from time to time as his duties permitted and now that Susana was finally back from Miami, he spent most of his spare time at the ranch with her. "Any excuse to avoid having to play golf," Susana teased him, although there was a grain of truth in that. But they did visit Wilfredo and Delia a couple of times, and despite her elegant coiffure and exquisite manicure, Susana was a good sport and a very accomplished guitarist. This little gently ageing group, ranging from fifty-five to sixty-three delighted in each other's company and the prospect of the forthcoming celebration of youth that was to be the wedding was anticipated with much joy and just a touch of wistfulness.

Miguel, Rafael's younger brother by two years, did not approve. He didn't approve of his brother, the Mayor, hobnobbing with these peasants or with the sole American who didn't live at El Dorado. "He thinks he's better than everyone else, living in that shack, never drinking in my bars or playing on my golf course!" Miguel would grumble to himself and he spat every time he sped past the faded red truck on the highway in his white Range Rover Evoque. "And the girl works as a maid here, for God's sake. It isn't dignified!" Miguel would complain out loud to himself whenever he saw Rosita on her way to clean apartments. The truth was Miguel was a petty snob and a jealous, lecherous fool. He was always ogling the young cleaning girls and had it not been for the abject fear of what his sharp-eyed, powerfully built Nicaraguan wife, Isabella, would do to him if she ever found out what a would-be philanderer he was, Miguel would surely have done more than just leer.

Rafael had given his brother the job as PR manager at El Dorado mostly because it kept him out of mischief and from causing too many problems for the family. There was a well-trained sales team for the resort, all bilingual, and even a small representative office in Miami. The extent of Miguel's responsibilities was meeting prospective clients at the airport and giving them a PowerPoint presentation, a few cocktails and a tour of the resort in a golf buggy. Even so, he still succeeded in putting a few live prospects off with his pompous manners, false charm and general loathsomeness.

This time however, a combination of his lust, his jealousy and the perceived opportunity to get one over on his golden brother and Tom, that uncouth hillbilly, combined to give him an idea. Sitting back in his red leather desk chair, rocking slightly back and forth with his hands steepled in front of him, Miguel decided to act.

Miguel was a short, pudgy man with thick black eyebrows and a ridiculously obvious toupée, which he bought online. The model was called, 'the Heartthrob'. Even if it had fitted well, it was still thirty years too young on him. However, his vanity knew few bounds, and his spiteful tongue and tyrannical manner towards the staff at El Dorado (over whom he had no direct authority but still, he was an Avila) meant that no one laughed to his face.

He had always been jealous of Rafael; his easy charm, his popularity, his success and his beautiful wife. But this time, he vowed to himself, he would make Rafa look like a fool. Miguel determined to wreck the wedding. It would serve that peasant girl right for having ideas above her station and embarrass the Mayor.

So Miguel concocted his plan. As his intellect was limited, so was his plot. He planned to get Jorge fired so the wedding would have to be postponed. Next, he planned to circulate the rumour that Rosa was sleeping with that damn gringo, Tom. That would fix it and make Rafael look like a naïve fool at the same time! Miguel picked up the phone on his desk and dialled the extension of Las Olas. "Chef Angelo! This is Avila. I think you could do with a night off!"

A few days before the wedding, Susana arrived unannounced and unaccompanied, and took Delia to one side. Half an hour later, she emerged from the little house and left. Delia spent the rest of the day humming to herself and when Wilfredo asked her what was going on, she merely winked and said, "You'll see!" Delia spent the next day whispering into the little mobile phone Susana had given her when no one was looking.

That same evening, Miguel invited the Martins to dinner at Las Olas. The Martins were a recently retired couple from Omaha who had sold their dry-cleaning business and with a modest but profitable portfolio and a reasonable annuity, they decided they wanted to buy a retirement condo somewhere warm, with a beach and it didn't really matter where. On more or less a whim, and after an evening in an expat advice chat room, they made arrangements to see four places on the Pacific coast. The first two were far too expensive, the next one had been perfect but too far from a hospital as Lucas Martin was diabetic and Mavis Martin had had a triple bypass a couple of years earlier. Their last port of call before returning to Nebraska was El Dorado. They had been quite impressed but after a long discussion, listing the pros and cons, they had decided to forego the Latin American plan and look into Hawaii. Besides, they couldn't wait to get away from that horrible little Mike person who had been clinging to them all day. But as the Martins were good, decent people they didn't want to offend the man, particularly as they were about to turn down the opportunity to spend $320,000 on a three-bedroom condo in the Casa Real complex. So, they accepted his invitation graciously and at eight o'clock the three sat down at Sr Avila's table in the tastefully decorated and surprisingly busy (for a Tuesday), Las Olas restaurant.

About the same time as the party of three were examining the menus, Tom pulled up outside in his truck. He had a cheque he wanted to give Jorge as a wedding present but he wanted to do it discreetly and not make a big deal of it. So, Tom figured he would catch him at work and avoid the fuss and grateful hugs. As he got out of the truck, Tom noticed the flashy white Evoque in the car park and always eager to avoid the reprehensible Mike, he walked round the back of the restaurant to where the kitchen door was ajar. Just as he was about to walk in and look for Jorge, he saw Miguel

Avila come into the kitchen. *No doubt to tell them how to do their job*, thought Tom grimly and decided to wait until the odious little twerp had gone. The waiters and the entire *brigade de cuisine* scattered leaving only Jorge standing with a ladle hovering a few inches above the lobster bisque which had come up a bit too thick and was now rapidly forming a skin.

"Ah, young Diaz! I hear it's quite a week for you, my boy! Head chef for the first time and getting married to boot! I just wanted to wish you luck in both endeavours! Such a lovely girl! Congratulations, my boy! My brother and all the family are so happy for you!" And with that, and before an astonished Jorge could utter no more than a strangulated thank you, Miguel put his short arms around the slender chef and hugged him, patting his back like a long absent relative at an airport reunion. Without another word, Miguel turned on his heel and walked briskly out of the kitchen back to the table as the startled kitchen staff filtered back to their stations.

What no one knew, what no one saw, was that in that moment of warmth and emotion, in that avuncular embrace, while Miguel was clasping Jorge to his bosom and clapping him firmly on the back, from his cupped palm a handful of small white pills fell silently into the rapidly thickening bisque. Well, almost no one saw. Tom pushed the kitchen back door open wide, brushed straight past poor Jorge, swiped the saucepan with the bisque off the hob and with the entire dumbstruck restaurant staff in tow, including the utterly bemused Jorge still clutching the ladle, marched through the swing doors into the main restaurant and right up to the farthest table from the kitchen. The table where Miguel, who sat open mouthed with his napkin tucked into the front of his shirt, and the startled Martins were seated. They were confronted with a tall man with wild white hair, a naked torso and no shoes banging a copper saucepan down onto the tablecloth, knocking over a glass of ice water as he did so.

"Sir, Madam, forgive the interruption," Tom said quietly. He didn't need to raise his voice; you could have heard a cotton bud drop let alone a pin. Indicating the pan with the lobster bisque, Tom directed his question at the Martins while Miguel sat absolutely motionless as if turned to stone. "I wonder if you wouldn't mind taking a peek in this saucepan for me and telling me if there is anything unusual in it?" The Martins both half stood up to peer into the pan. While Lucas Martin squinted through his glasses, Mavis, who had very pretty and very sharp green eyes exclaimed, "Why there, on the surface, it looks like a tablet."

Unfortunately for Miguel, his interruption of Jorge's work in the kitchen a few moments ago had so shocked the young chef that the bisque remained unstirred and the skin had indeed formed. Half submerged in this yellowy-orange skin, the pretty green eagle eyes of Mavis Martin had discerned a small white pill.

"Thank you, so much. Sorry for the interruption and please enjoy your meal. Young Jorge here is an excellent chef," Tom said graciously and picking up the saucepan with one hand and grasping Miguel by the elbow with the other, he made an irresistible suggestion that the two go for a little walk. Miguel stood up, as if in a trance, and allowed himself to be shepherded into the parking lot.

Inside, it was the young chef who regained his composure first and in excellent, although heavily accented English, as the usual din of a busy restaurant returned, he personally went through the menu with the Martins who were charmed by Jorge's demeanour. They went for the clam chowder.

"What was it, Mikey? Laxatives, sleeping pills? You slimy bastard. I don't know whether to kick your ass or call your brother. Maybe I should do both."

"Take your hands off me, you oaf! Who do you th—"

"I'd stop right there, Miguelito. We both know you slipped those pills into the bisque. What did you want to do, get Jorge fired? Force them to postpone the wedding? Make your brother look foolish?"

"I don't know what you are talking about, you must be drunk," Miguel protested but even he wasn't convinced by his own phoney outrage.

"Well, you won't mind having a taste of this delicious bisque now, will you?" said Tom as he grabbed Miguel by the throat and brought the saucepan towards his face until it was an inch from Miguel's quivering lips.

"Ok, ok! Enough, enough! What are you going to do?" There was no more defiance in the voice now, just a hint of a whine. Tom lowered the saucepan and poured the contents over Miguel's shoes.

"I am going to be nice, Mikey, nicer than you know how to be. I will forget everything I saw tonight and we can just say I was a bit tipsy and was playing a joke on you if that will save your fat face. But you have to do something for me, agreed?"

Miguel opened his mouth to say something but just exhaled, looked down at his bisque-coated alligator shoes and nodded.

"Good boy! Now listen…"

The wedding day dawned bright and warm with a slight breeze off the ocean making it bearable rather than oppressive, and the wedding party and most of Santa Maria walked to the little church. Everyone was there since practically the whole family on both sides lived within ten miles. Tom and Mabel were present and Tom was even wearing a white linen suit, although he still wore his uncomfortable green deck shoes as a gesture of defiance. Rafael and Susana Avila arrived unfashionably on time in an old Toyota so as not to steal any scenes and Wilfredo, the happiest man and the proudest father, gave his beautiful Rosita away to her beloved Jorge.

The reception was due to take place in the cantina right in the middle of the village and as bride, groom and father of the bride set off on the short walk from the church everyone else stopped.

"Mama?" asked Rosa with a note of concern.

Suddenly with a blast of horns that would have saved Joshua some time at Jericho, three brightly painted old American school buses pulled up and led by Tom and Mabel, everyone got on as if it were rehearsed. Everyone that is, except Wilfredo, Jorge and Rosa who all looked as if the world had gone mad.

"Come, Fredo," said the Mayor gently taking his friend by the arm as Susana and Delia guided the newlyweds away from the cantina.

"This is our wedding present to you."

Wilfredo, Delia and Susana took a seat on of the bus which Wilfredo now noticed had been decked out in ribbons and the Mayor of San Lorenzo himself guided Rosa and Jorge into the front seats and took his own place at the wheel and with a loud honk of the horn, the convoy set off for the El Dorado Country Club, the most lavish resort in the province if not the entire country. Twenty loud minutes later, the merry trio of buses pulled into the car park of the El Dorado.

No expense had been spared. The Mayor had laid on everything from lobster and champagne to smoked salmon and the biggest wedding cake anyone had seen for many years. There were the inevitable, glorious fireworks and a live band (and obviously the karaoke machine as well) and the party lasted until three in the morning.

The biggest surprise came the next day when Jorge and Rosita awoke from their first night together as man and wife in the newly and beautifully refurbished house;

166

Jorge saw that his car, his late father's 1978 orange Datsun Cherry had disappeared and in its place was a brand new blue Honda Accord. Delighted and surprised Jorge and Rosa danced around the car while barefoot children ran around them shrieking with laughter. A few hours later, Jorge drove Rosa to the Mayor's office and asked to see Sr Avila. Presently the Mayor, looking a little hungover came down to greet them rather than ask for them to be sent up, and was taken aback to be hugged by Jorge and receive kisses all over his cheeks from Rosa.

"What on earth is the matter? Are you two still drunk?" asked the Mayor in confusion.

"Sr Mayor, we just had to come and say thank you. Thank you so much for such a wonderful wedding present. It's such a lovely colour!" said Rosa half laughing, half crying with joy.

"What is? What's a lovely colour? I don't understand."

"The car! Your wedding present!" the newlyweds exclaimed as one.

"My dear children! I have absolutely no idea what you are talking about!"

Four months later, three men are sitting in a beautiful newly-built wooden Dory fishing boat. The man at the oars is tall, with wild white hair, bare-chested and smoking a pipe. The man in the prow, gazing intently at his line with the practised eye of an expert, pushes his battered straw hat back on his head and breathes in the ocean breeze as if drinking the sweetest of wines. The third man, wearing jeans and somewhat incongruously, cowboy boots is pouring something we suspect is not coffee from a flask into an elegant small solid silver cup.

"So, my friends, we have been on this exquisite new boat made by a true craftsman and an honorary San Lorenzan. That is Fredo's pleasure. Next time we must go to my ranch and spend the day in the saddle. That is my pleasure. And Sr Tom, what would be your pleasure?"

"Well, Your Honour, what would you say to a round of golf?"

THE INTERPRETERS

Early one Sunday morning, during the height of summer, Pascal Cheung was hot and flustered, and enduring a barrage of abuse from the small crowd gathered round the open hatch of the Angel Mart. Volley after volley of insults and wagging fingers were directed towards his sweating face from the angry and exasperated group standing in the dust outside the tiny shop, which was in effect, two twenty-foot containers knocked into one, painted red with white lettering in the classic Coca-Cola style announcing that Angel Mart was open and were purveyors of drinks, ice and general groceries. Pascal felt frustrated, angry, hurt and very confused all at the same time. His one consolation, ironically, was also the reason the mini mob was so angry; he couldn't understand a word they were saying.

For Pascal Cheung spoke no Spanish at all. And for a shopkeeper in the only store for nine miles in any direction in an insignificant northern province of an oft-overlooked Central American backwater, not speaking Spanish was a distinct handicap.

In truth, Pascal was neither the owner nor the regular manager of the Angel Mart. That was his son, Henri. But Henri was back in Hong Kong having been refused a renewal of his residency due to a technicality.

The technicality being he hadn't come up with the $5000 necessary to get the visa officer at the consulate to overlook his criminal record again and grant him a further four years. The crimes for which Henri had a record were minor and were more transgressions of youth; joyriding in a stolen Volkswagen Beetle and stealing a goat, albeit a goat that belonged to a Hong Kong government official when the Union Jack still flew over Government House (that rather modest looking colonial building facing Victoria Peak on the main island). However, Señor Canto, the visa officer at the consulate was not interested in the severity of Henri Cheung's crimes. He was solely interested in when the $5000 could be discreetly handed over, in cash and naturally, out of office hours. So, Henri was stuck in the New Territories driving a cab with four cell phones attached to his dashboard, each of which represented the lines of communication to the various pies in which he had his desperate fingers in order to earn the money as quickly as possible. His current pies included the taxi, a water-cooler maintenance enterprise, a courier service and a failing tourism venture to give tours of the bay and the islands by boat. This latter undertaking, which he got into with his cousin, Lee, was failing for one clearly identifiable reason: the Canton Rose, the motorised junk which the cousins hoped would gain them their fortune, had been deemed unseaworthy by the harbour authorities and at the present moment was also impounded due to an outstanding tax demand.

Thus, the unfortunate Henri was scrabbling for every last cent (and losing most of it by his persistent gambling) so that he could return to his red-painted shack in the middle of a forgotten province miles from the shining ocean-front towns populated with retired Americans and gleaming shopping plazas. His beloved Angel Mart which, despite being not much more than a tin shed (which suffocated the occupants in summer and drove them half insane with the unending hours of tropical rain drumming on the metal roof during wet season) with half a dozen small refrigerator cabinets and a few shelves, which looked like they had been made from Meccano, was nevertheless a very profitable venture since the nearest competition was thirty-five minutes away on the infrequent and unreliable bus service along a dust-choked road in summer and a treacherous slick of mud in the rainy season. Besides, even if the local population in the village of San Juan and the neighbouring hamlets of San Pedro and La Virgen did catch the bus to the coastal retirement resort of Santa Cruz, peopled principally by Canadians, Americans and oddly enough, Belgians over sixty years old, some twelve miles away with its brand new and haughtily named, Mall de Las Americas, they could only go to see the Mall as a modern wonder, a tourist attraction, rather than as a retail experience since they were victims of the economic apartheid so prevalent in that part of the world. In the decent restaurants and outlets, malls, clinics and even cemeteries, the local people would be

the ones making great efforts to provide outstanding
service in return for perhaps the hope of a one dollar tip
from a wealthy foreigner. Yet none of these locals could
dream of eating or shopping or being seen by a doctor or
even being buried in these exclusive venues. "It is as if we
are not the owners of our own country," was the general
lament and such sentiment had propelled the former
communist-backed guerrilla leader and ex-dockworker,
Horatio Dominguez, to the presidency some twelve
years before but under whose auspices the expansion of
the 'gringo' towns had doubled and inflation now ran at
an uncomfortable 27%. However, Horatio had the knack
of staying in power thanks to an irresistible combination
of several phenomena: intimidating his equally corrupt
political rivals; lengthy vocal rants every month on the
radio (still the only form of mass communication that
reached the provinces since the internet, mobile phone
coverage and cable TV were unaffordable and largely
inaccessible thirty miles outside the capital and two of
the larger provincial cities and, of course, the expatriate
populated resorts) railing against the moral decay of
capitalism, imperialism and other equally abhorrent
"isms"; free and equal education and healthcare to all
citizens (and true enough, education and healthcare
were free, mostly because there was less than 4% of the
budget directed into them and equal because they were
equally awful no matter where you were in the country);
and finally, and most significantly, the unadvertised
and immense income diligently raised and judiciously

allotted from the vast amount of drugs, arms, luxury goods and even people trafficked through the borders. The President and his henchmen had, of course, never been involved in any illicit trade themselves but the unofficial levies raised on the thousands of shipments known to most people as the 'Look-the-other-way Tax', provided what Interpol suggested could be as much as 60% of GDP.

So even as Henri juggled phone calls while negotiating traffic and terrifying his Dutch tourist passengers on the way to see the Tian Tan Buddha at the Po Lin Monastery, all he could think of was returning to his tin goldmine in the back of beyond and worry what was happening to his business left in the less than capable hands of his seventy-two-year-old father, Pascal.

Here it might be well to explain how the Cheungs had the decidedly un-Chinese forenames of Pascal and Henri. Well, to understand that, one must consider the unusually high number of retired Belgians in the country. And that is directly a result of the 'Scramble for Africa' in the final decades of the nineteenth and opening decade of the twentieth centuries.

When Leopold I, King of the Belgians, hatched his outlandish plot to gain a colony for his country and the concomitant wealth and fame, his beady eye cast around the globe for a suitable colonial candidate. Having discreetly enquired into a possible purchase of various territories including the Philippines from the Spanish and several islands from Britain, Leopold decided to concentrate his efforts on the vast Congo basin in Africa but not before a little known venture in Central America. During his father's time, a disastrous attempt had been made to colonise a portion of Guatemala. This venture lasted some fourteen years before yellow fever and malaria carried off most of the settlers and any mention of the region slipped quietly into obscurity. So, although you will find documentation of the Guatemalan venture during the reign of Leopold I, only a very few have ever heard of Leopold II's dalliance in Latin America in the final years of the nineteenth century. It was never official, never sanctioned and so when, inevitably, it failed after nine years, no one really noticed except the three thousand 'colonists' and their families and servants, most of whom, although better defended from malaria due to quinine, were left to make their way back to Belgium, or anywhere, unaided, bankrupt and forgotten, or stay and forge some sort of life, or simply rot. However, the early years of the adventure were a whirl of construction, over optimistic reporting on natural resources and exuberance that Belgium was taking its rightful place in the brotherhood of empires with the savage world carved up into coloured slices each according to their colonial masters; red for Britain, blue for France and so on.

In a mad undertaking such as this, perhaps the maddest thing of all was the 'Railway under the Volcano'; a bold or rather, reckless attempt to build a railway line from Colombia to Texas irrespective of the terrain. The

Belgian general, General Claude Letruc, in charge of the project, being rather linear of disposition, declared that the shortest route through the territory under his command was directly north. A laudable conclusion and only flawed in that this direct route would take the railway not only through some of the densest rainforest north of the Amazon but would also necessitate the track being lain either over, under or through several dormant and a couple of not so dormant volcanic craters. The fact that two hundred and fifty miles of track had been laid before this inconvenient truth was discovered can only be put down to an unfortunate oversight. If you take a guide, a jeep and a stout pair of walking boots, you can still see where the tracks end, all too abruptly at the shore of a sulphuric pool in the ash rich foothills of Mount Ah Chuy Kak. The name was Mayan and was the name of the god of war and destruction, so that gives you an idea into the general hostility of the environment.

However, in those heady jingoistic days of the Belle Époque, nothing prevented the sense of Belgian manifest destiny or the importation of unpaid and coerced 'volunteers' from Africa, and miserably paid and appallingly treated Chinese workers whose fathers had slaved and died to help bring the railroads across the United States, to now help forge a new railway for a brand new colony between the Pacific and Atlantic oceans linking north to south in a lucrative iron corridor of trade.

Of course, it was doomed and its inevitable failure

was the prevailing mood the year Michelle Audan met Li Han Cheung who followed the Asian labour gangs and was employed as an interpreter by the local bosses since he not only spoke his native Cantonese but also Mandarin, Siamese, Vietnamese and English. Li had come from a poor family but with determination and his linguistic gift, he had climbed out of his father's fishing smack back in Hong Kong and into the Imperial diplomatic service. In his travels in the capacity of little more than a talented servant but first-class discreet interpreter, he travelled to Europe (where he added some French and Spanish to his repertoire) and later to America where he absconded and got a job with a railroad company as a liaison between the American overseers and the Chinese labourers, which gave him grudging respect from both and affection from neither. Growing tired of this climate of poverty and not belonging, Li heard that a large contingent of Hong Kong Chinese were bound for the new Belgian would-be colony in the jungles of Central America and duly set off to make his fortune. With a forged letter of recommendation from the non-existent Secretary of Linguistic Affairs of the United States of America, he secured an interview with General Letruc and rather than be appointed as official interpreter, Li managed to create a role and title for himself as general manager of the Asian contingent of the Belgian Imperial project in the fledgling colony of San Cristobal. What that really meant was that he was made the Belgians chief go-between with the Chinese workforce. A task made somewhat trickier than almost exactly the same job he had had in America due to the fact that slavery was officially illegal (although this was largely ignored by the Belgians) and the Chinese were supposed to actually receive payment for their labour. However at a meeting between Li, General Letruc and a lean government lawyer from Antwerp called Cornelius Neeskens, an elaborate set of rules and charges was established by which the Chinese workers were paid 8 Cristobals (the newly introduced colonial currency and utterly worthless) a day. However, their room and board in the 50-man leaky wooden shack accommodation provided by the Belgian employers cost 5 Cristobals a day and the rest they were allowed to spend as they pleased. The fact was that the currency was unconvertible and the only place the Chinese could spend their remaining 3 Cristobals was either in the shop and canteen run by the administration or in Li Han's little bar. This enterprising and lucrative side-line was no more than a large wooden shed with a few mah-jong sets and the nastiest cheapest whisky that Li could buy for next to nothing from the Mexican schooners that occasionally called into the one functioning port some three day's mule ride from the railroad administration centre.

As Belgium's dream of Latin American riches and railways entered its decline, accelerated by the newly exploited riches in The Congo, Li was quite a wealthy man having expanded his gut-rot saloon into a whore house for the Americans who had swooped in to prospect in the volcanic rivers in what was a short-lived, violent and ultimately abandoned gold-rush. The madam of this shanty bordello was Michelle Audan, born in Liege and former mistress of a Belgian officer who had died of dysentery after three months in San Cristobal and who had been obliged to make ends meet by discreetly entertaining those officers whose wives had not yet, or never would make the journey from the Belgian motherland. As those colonists who had not succumbed to disease, madness or desertion began to leave by whatever means they could and return unsung and unknown to Brussels and beyond, Michelle found that her health and looks had faded to such an extent that she could no longer seduce her passage back to Europe and at that moment, in her hour of desperate need, she met Li Han. Li was just in the process of building his brothel which was to be 'staffed' by a few local fallen women (the nineteenth century term for a single mother), several opium-smoking Vietnamese girls, an Austrian seamstress who made the dresses and who drank gin in frightening quantities and a 'Scottish' woman called Blanche who had a different story of her origins for every client. In fact, Blanche was born and raised in San Cristobal to an indigenous mother who had a fling with a Jesuit called Graham from Ayr during a moment of weakness, which he realised was a crisis of the soul and who promptly hanged himself out of guilt and after consuming almost a gallon of rum. Li realised that beating alone would not keep the girls in check so he offered Michelle a home and the position of madam and in return, Michelle agreed to marry Li and this marriage of seedy convenience actually grew into one of genuine affection and one unexpected result of the union was a baby boy whom Michelle insisted be given her father's name, Henri.

Sadly, the Hans bliss did not last all that long. When Henri was nine years old, his mother died of an unidentified disease and Li lost heart, sold his business at a huge loss to the Mayor of San Cristobal which was shortly to be renamed Independencia and where today an overgrown Belgian cemetery can still be found. With the money, he bought passage for himself and Henri, and sailed for his native Hong Kong with his little boy that same year. Li Han did not survive the voyage probably dying of the same disease that had claimed his wife and was buried at sea, in case it was contagious. His son, Henri arrived in Hong Kong for the first time in his life, aged ten with a handful of his mother's fake jewels and his father's jade ring in his pockets, a few clothes tied up in a sheet and a book in French given to him by his mother on his ninth birthday. The book, which he could read as fluently as he could Cantonese, was Voltaire's *Candide*.

It is ironic to think today that the significant number of Belgians who have retired to the land (although they are overwhelmingly in the coastal resorts rather than the region around Independencia) of tropical heat, low taxation and American-staffed private health clinics and a land for which those few who know the story feel a sentimental attachment, are treading in the footsteps of so many of their compatriots who perished in the 'stinking jungles and swamps of benighted San Cristobal'.

Henri Cheung, only son of the late Li Han and Michelle Cheung now found himself an oddity in a strange land. With his Chinese facial features inherited from his father but with his mother's blue eyes and mousey brown hair, he found it hard to be accepted totally either by the Chinese or the Europeans. However, as he spoke French, Spanish and Cantonese and a few words of English, his skills were always in demand. Li Han had a brother, Bao Zhi who owned a chain of large laundries, which serviced several embassies and the grander of the hotels. Bao was an irascible, avaricious and very cunning man who had made a modest fortune from his forty years washing others people's dirty linen. He had made good. Coming from nothing and by sheer will and ruthless determination, Bao now lived in a two-storey house in Kowloon with his own servants. Nevertheless, Bao Zhi had loved his brother and so, when his ten-year-old orphaned nephew appeared, lost and distraught over his parents' death, Bao took him in with open arms and treated him as if he were his own son. This kindness was returned doubly by the love and respect Bao Zhi received from Henri, and equally rewardingly by the increased business that his polyglot nephew brought in as he could negotiate directly with the British hotel managers and the French speaking diplomatic staff in the embassies.

Henri was a diligent and valuable member of Bao Zhi's staff and Bao, who had been 'cursed' with five daughters and no sons, was nearing eighty years old as Henri turned thirty, had decided to retire and hand the business to his favoured nephew. By this time, Henri had been married three times; his first wife dying in childbirth with their third son and his second wife, having born four more children, two boys and two girls, had been run over by a British Army staff car whose driver had a heart attack at the wheel. His third wife, Ah Lam, who was the daughter of a Chinese doctor and who had been trained as a nurse, was clever and pretty and a devoted mother to her seven step-children and her own baby daughter, and was proud of her husband who was about to become a very wealthy man indeed.

Just as everything seemed to be in place to guarantee a happy and comfortable life for Henri's clan, misfortune intervened with devastating effects. Bao Zhi died suddenly and disastrously for Henri, without writing down in his will that which he had often discussed with his nephew. Although a few weeks shy of his eightieth birthday, Bao was wiry and strong and in excellent health. The suspicion is that one or more of his five daughters poisoned him in order to prevent Henri taking over the business. Nothing was ever proved and Henri's cousins claimed the business and merely offered him a job managing the major customers but no share in the business, which his uncle had wished him to inherit.

Poor Henri! Eight children, and with Ah Lam five

months pregnant with her second and his ninth child, he was turfed out of his home by the sisters who took possession of Bao Zhi's house for their own offspring. Although Henri had been careful with money and had a tidy sum put by, he reasoned that supporting a wife and soon-to-be nine children and finding somewhere to live was going to be a struggle unless he took some drastic action. The drastic action he took was to forsake the land of his ancestors and return to the land of his birth.

Six months later, Henri, Ah Lam and eight children (the passage proved a rough one and Ah Lam's new baby boy died on board after just two days and joined his paternal grandfather, Li Han in an ocean grave) were settling into a new life some two hundred miles from the former Belgian enclave of San Cristobal. Henri had used the bulk of his life's savings, which was enough to pay the passage and buy a surprisingly spacious but rather run down two-storey building in a shabby area of the city but one just a five-minute walk from the Plaza General Menendez. The General was actually an escaped murderer and horse thief who had jumped on the opportunistic bandwagon of the fight for liberty from Spanish rule stirred up by Simon Bolivar in the 1820s. Along with his unsavoury band of cutthroats and ne'er-do-wells, Pablo Menendez had seen the struggle for nationhood as a perfect chance to get rich quick and exploit the general chaos. He became a hero of the nascent republic when he single-handedly brought down the cruel and corrupt Spanish governor, Diego

Jesus Valdez de Jimenez, as he attempted to flee the country to enlist the help of Prussian mercenaries, who were between wars at that time and relaxing in Antigua, to come and crush this impertinent uprising and exact terrible revenge for defying Spanish rule. What actually happened is that the Governor was desperately trying to get to the coast with his wife and daughter, three servants and a chest of golden coins so that they could go to the United States where he hoped to buy a cattle ranch.

Unfortunately, Diego's coach sustained a broken axle bumping across a dry river bed just as Pablo and his gang, on their way to the capital to see what pillage and plunder might be on offer, were settling down to camp for the night on the opposite bank. The three servants fled into the scrub, the gold was taken and the wife and daughter raped and shot by the gang. Pablo Menendez himself slit the governor's throat and removed his little finger on which he wore the signet ring of the Imperial Court and thus became a national hero. He probably could have even been the second president of the country had the founding president of the republic, Oscar Martinez, not decided to make himself president for life and have Pablo and a sundry collection of other popular figures, intellectuals and military men shot for treason before he himself was thrown off the balcony of the presidential palace by a lawyer called Hernando Borosa, (the man who *did* become the second president of the republic, for about three months).

The Plaza General Menendez was where most of the

embassies were in the capital and Henri thought if he had been so successful using his languages and business skills in his uncle's laundries back in Hong Kong, then there was nothing stopping him doing the same thing here. Only this time, as sole owner, he would see his large family secure and wealthy with their fate in their own hands. And now, fortune smiled on the Cheungs and Henri, with the help of the saintly Ah Lam and his eight boisterous children, forged a new life and a successful business providing laundry services for a dozen embassies and consulates, three major hotels and even the presidential palace for state dinners and other grand occasions.

By the outbreak of the Second World War, Henri had moved out of the second storey of their first home, which he had bought some eight years previously, and into a lilac-painted house with a large garden in the affluent suburb of Miraflores (and there is hardly a single capital city in the whole of Latin America that *doesn't* have a wealthy suburb called Miraflores) and had three laundries managed by his older children, and those of his children still of school age were studying at the private Academia San Ignacio. The entire family had converted to Catholicism and spoke Spanish in society but enjoyed delicious Cantonese food and cheerful Chinese chatter at home and all the children learned English at school. An extra blessing in the form of a son arrived in November 1941. He was the youngest child by some ten years but was the absolute apple of his father's eye and

Henri felt his life was complete. All his other children had Chinese names (and typical Chinese features save the girls who had blue eyes) but since his youngest child had been born, as he had, far from Hong Kong in the land where Henri's Belgian mother had eventually fallen in love with his father, Henri insisted in giving the boy a name from his mother's side of the family. So, it was that little Pascal, named for his grandmother's brother who had been a baker in Liege and who had died aged forty from syphilis, was baptised in the church of San Francisco one sunny Sunday morning with the scent of magnolias hanging sweetly in the still, warm air. It was a Sunday to remember. It was the 7th December 1941: the day the Japanese bombed Pearl Harbour.

In 1938 there had been, coincidentally, general elections in two neighbouring and often antipathetic countries. To the north in Santa Elena, a 'populist' government modelled on the Fasciti in Italy, complete with its own mini Mussolini, President General Florian Gatillo (and having a surname that means trigger was apt as the Generalissimo went everywhere with a pair of silver Colt revolvers on his hips which he had a tendency to use indiscriminately) had bullied his way to power with the help of thuggery and Italian money, and the new government was planning to convert the long-disputed port of Buenafortuna into a naval base at the disposal of friendly Axis powers. Buenafortuna was right on the border between Santa Elena and the land in which poor Pascal had so recently been born; the two countries had fought several skirmishes and two outright wars over the last hundred years for its ownership. Buenafortuna had changed flags so many times that in 1936, the then governor of the province, Hector Bartolo, went to Washington DC and asked the Americans to intervene to stop the dispute and guarantee the independence and safety of the lands and peoples in his region in return for granting the Americans the right to keep a permanent garrison in the city and a few gunboats in the port as well as a lucrative trade monopoly for the excellent bananas produced in the region. The Americans agreed but did not act with any particular urgency, so by the time the Americans sent one civilian vessel with an advance party of sixteen soldiers from the Quartermaster Corps, armed only with service revolvers, the new government of General Gatillo had seized full control of Buenafortuna and rumour has it that the General himself dispatched the well-meaning and unfortunate Governor Bartolo with a single bullet in the eye. The Americans were treated kindly and with due dignity but after two days were politely but firmly shown the door and withdrew to whence they had sailed. At about the same time, to the south, the old enemy of Santa Elena chose its new president. An American-educated, millionaire Baptist and a disciple of Henry Ford won a landslide with over 80% of the vote and in his native region bordering Buenafortuna, some say over 100%. President Manuel Cordoba promised to put meat on the table, halve the price of tortillas and provide jobs to all men over fifteen and make his nation proud once more. Of course, none of these things came to pass but it made a great election campaign. Practically the first thing President Cordoba did was cable his millionaire industrialist friends in the USA and within three weeks, a flotilla of one warship, six gunboats and several ancillary vessels steamed into the small harbour at Chichamura some five miles down the coast from Buenafortuna.

It was all quite simple and almost bloodless. President Cordoba's friends and sponsors back in Washington passed a House Resolution recognising the historical right to the city and port of Buenafortuna and despite protestations from the Italian, German, Spanish, Japanese and of course, Santa Elena governments and the shooting of an American navy doctor in the arm (the doctor just happened to be out collecting butterflies on the border) by a local farmer who thought he was after his chickens, the Americans took possession of Buenafortuna in the name of President Cordoba and his noble people in August 1939.

By 1942, Buenafortuna was a heavily fortified city with 1,200 American troops and several destroyers, and it commanded a strategically vital position between North and South America. Santa Elena was thus rendered neutral and contributed nothing to the Axis war effort save a tranquil holiday resort for Italian officers and deserters. To this day, the best pasta in the Americas can be found in Santa Elena.

So President Cordoba had his beloved port back and

had the comfort of a large and friendly force of United States soldiers and marines on his doorstep. Rather too friendly given the alarming rise in cases of gonorrhoea and the dark-skinned children with blue eyes born in the area until 1960, when the six-term sixty-six-year-old President Cordoba, wearing black silk stockings and a red corset, had a stroke while being flogged by his valet, Felipe and the Americans in turn were expelled by the newly 'elected' People's Revolutionary Party of Alfredo Gozo who claimed Buenafortuna in the name of the people and set about turning it into the largest drug trafficking port between Cali and Miami, in the name of the people, naturally.

The disastrous side effect on the Cheung family of this political situation and the arrival of the Americans in 1939 was not felt until seventeen days after Pascal was baptised and the Japanese flattened Pearl Harbour when President Cordoba issued a decree expelling all German, Italian and Japanese citizens or those of such descent going back three generations and the repossession of their assets for use in the fight against the powers of totalitarianism. Some 4500 bewildered people found themselves one intensely hot New Year's Day morning on the quay at Buenafortuna being loaded like cattle onto four freighters bound for Spain. Two of the freighters never made it, torpedoed by U-boats, victims of mistaken identity. One limped into Cadiz three weeks later with several hundred passengers stricken with typhoid and the fourth, for reasons only known to the captain, landed in Luanda, capital of the Portuguese colony of Angola. Baby Pascal Cheung was on board this boat along with his father, mother and eight brothers and sisters. None of the Cheung children had married and the oldest boy, Wei-Shan who was 22 was quite relieved to be leaving as he had just found out his girlfriend, Frida, the sixteen-year-old daughter of a Swiss hotel manager and his Venezuelan wife, was two months pregnant. As it turned out, he needn't have worried since Frida's parents decided to take the family to Argentina a month later and were killed when their ship hit a mine in the River Plate. Despite frenzied protestations to the Ministry of Justice, the US Embassy and the British Consulate and showing passports and birth certificates to prove that he was not of Japanese citizenship or descent, Henri Cheung was told he and his family would have to leave. In truth, the deputy Minister in charge of the newly created department of Alien Affairs, Rolando Garcia knew full well the Cheungs' antecedence but they looked so 'oriental' and therefore could not be trusted. Besides, Rolando had an eye on the Cheungs' lilac house with the pretty garden for his mistress, Hortense who was born in Alsace to a German mother and a French father who later became an official in the Vichy government but whose loyalty was beyond question once she became Rolando's paramour. In March 1945 after Hortense suddenly died of a burst appendix, they found a radio set hidden in one of her hatboxes which she had regularly used throughout the final three years of the war to communicate with Berlin. Rolando took the news badly but rather than marching out to the pretty garden of the lilac-painted house and doing the honourable thing with a revolver, he fled over the border disguised as a nun and ran a religious bookshop in Santa Elena until he died in 1957.

It took the Cheung family over three years to reach Hong Kong. Of the eleven family members who landed at Luanda in late January 1942, nine reached Hong Kong in May 1945. From Luanda, they trekked to Johannesburg and then onto Cape Town where they settled for a time among the small Chinese community and Henri, who had managed to smuggle a few thousand dollars aboard the ship which was enough to encourage the captain to sail towards the relative safety of Africa, opened a restaurant which just about kept their heads above water. Sadly, in early 1944, Henri died from a blood clot on the brain that was thought to have been caused from a fall from a stepladder while changing a light bulb in the restaurant. Ah Lam heroically kept the restaurant open and her brood fed and clothed for two more years at great cost to her health, but managed to return with her family to Hong Kong on a Chinese cargo ship whose captain had been a frequent diner at the restaurant. Wei-Shan stayed on in Cape Town and kept the restaurant, married the daughter of a tailor from Shanghai and raised a family. Ah Lam and her eight children, having landed in Hong Kong, were able to stay with the captain of the cargo ship who was very fond of Henri's oldest daughter, Wu-Han, whom he eventually married and the Cheung family went back into the laundry business again albeit in a very small way. By 1960, Ah Lam was able to reflect on a very successful fifteen years as owner of three small laundries, mother-in-law six times over, with two weddings on the horizon and grandmother to seventeen. When Pascal married aged eighteen, Ah Lam retired and signed her business over to her children and went back to Cape Town to live with Wei-Shan and his wife and five children, and to be near her beloved Henri, who was buried in the Chinese cemetery on Signal Hill. Pascal, Ah Lam's only natural son, was a sweet-natured, rather shy child who was not particularly blessed with brains or good looks and was often bullied at school and never fought back. Thankfully, several of his older siblings ensured that Pascal was left alone most of the time. Showing no particular aptitude for school, or much social grace, or any of the Cheung entrepreneurial spirit, Ah Lam would often despair about the fate of her youngest child. The best she could hope for, she often said to herself, was that he would settle down to a job in one of her laundries, perhaps delivering clean sheets to the few guest houses that were customers and maybe marry a nice, dim-witted girl who would look after him and know that he would not beat her. The only discernable talent that Pascal displayed was carving wood.

He started whittling when he was very small and by the time he was eight made his own wooden toys;

soldiers, a little sailing boat and presents for his older brothers and sisters and little baby cousins from pencil boxes to elaborate, gaily painted dolls and spinning tops. When Pascal was sixteen, he was out one day taking a parcel of freshly laundered sheets to a small inn frequented by commercial salesmen from the mainland, when he met the hostel owner's daughter, Chan-Juan, who was almost fifteen and who had been born with a dark purple birthmark covering almost half of her face. Pascal didn't even notice the birthmark; he was enraptured by Chan-Juan's smile and her silvery laugh. As soon as Chang-Juan turned seventeen, they married with the full blessing and to the great relief of both mothers-in-law. Pascal delivered the laundry and Chan-Juan, who was a superb cook worked as a chef for the Hong Kong Police.

Three years after they married, a son was born. Pascal carved the crib himself and the little boy was named in honour of his late father, Henri. Pascal continued working in what had become his brothers' and sisters' business and although technically he owned a small share in the family business, his mother granted full authority over his finances to his siblings on condition that they always look out for him. In their spare time, Pascal and Chan-Juan would play with little Henri and his collection of wooden toys, all exquisitely made by his father, and although not rich, not educated and not sophisticated, they were a very happy family unit. Little Henri turned out to be a precocious child and somewhat boisterous; often in trouble for being cheeky at school or stealing apples, getting into fights with boys twice his age and size in the neighbourhood or being caught playing dice in the street with drunken English sailors on shore leave. Henri had a great ear for languages and learned Spanish and French from his uncles and aunts and amused his parents with his skill in mimicry and accents. By the time he was thirteen; Henri could drink a pot of rum or smoke a pipe with the sailors while cracking risqué jokes in English and winning their money with loaded dice. But somehow, having inherited his father's sweet disposition and his mother's winning smile, Henri never quite got into the amount of grief he really deserved.

So life continued and the Cheungs laughed, cried, celebrated, commiserated, enjoyed and endured as all families do. The year Henri turned seventeen, Chan-Juan developed a fever, a day later she slipped into a coma and two days after that, she died. The cause of the fever was never established and the disconsolate Pascal nearly took his own life. As it was, he wandered around the streets for days in a fog of grief, which ended in a very badly broken leg when he fell down a flight of steps. The leg really needed a pin but Pascal didn't want one so when the plaster came off, he walked with a severe limp from that day. His brothers and sisters made sure he had money and one of his nieces or nephews would bring him a hot meal every day but Pascal retreated from the world and sat in his little parlour carving: no longer toys but strange, abstract figures reminiscent of swans or dolphins, or bizarrely shaped trees whose beautiful tortured forms were captivating yet eluded interpretation. No one who happened to drop by to visit Pascal was unaffected by the almost surreal carvings and all agreed that just when you thought you had grasped the meaning behind one, a flicker of a candle in the room, or a breath of wind or the slightest tilt of the head changed the dynamic of the wood and the moment of illumination was lost.

Young Henri could see that he was the last of his father's worries and ever gracious, took no offense, so one day a few months after his mother's death, Henri kissed Pascal on the forehead and took his leave of Hong Kong, having got himself a job as a cabin boy on a British cruise ship, and sailed away to Australia where he spent the next seven years living on his wits and mostly, just within the law. At various times he was a tour guide, a croupier in a casino (but the temptation was too great for him not to spend all his money after his shift), a jade dealer, a medical orderly and finally a car dealer. It was this last job that caused him to leave Adelaide in something of a hurry when the police were investigating several complaints of cars whose milometers had been tampered with. Henri signed up on a Liberian-registered container ship, the *Spirit of Colchis,* whose captain paid next to nothing but asked no questions, a sort of merchant marine version of the French Foreign Legion. Since the captain of the ship, a Lebanese called Mook, spoke only French, Arabic and a few words of English, Henri with his fluent but rather vulgar English and his Cantonese, French and Spanish was of great use to Captain Mook and served as radio operator and interpreter on board for two years. During that time he had no home and spent only enough time on land to get a girl, get a meal, find a card game and usually get into some sort of trouble with an angry husband or father, or bar owner or gambling creditor.

Henri was almost thirty years old when the *Spirit of Colchis* was steaming leakily away from its latest port of call in Havana, and he was sitting with Mook one evening playing chess over an enamel mug of rum, smoking a smuggled Montecristo. As usual, Captain Mook spoke French and Henri answered in English.

"Just one more stop on this trip, and then the owners are scrapping the tub. We are to make for Montevideo after this and the breaking yard. The crew is to be paid off and dispersed and you and I have been offered a job on an oil tanker in Alaska." Mook shivered and spat, then sighed and blew a forlorn smoke ring.

Henri never looked at charts or manifests and barely noticed where they were unless it was somewhere with pretty girls, cheap booze and saps to fleece at dice or cards.

"Fuck that! I'm not freezing my bollocks off on some floating time bomb! Anyway where is this final stop before the knacker's yard? We should make it a real swansong to remember!"

"Oh we can have a party alright, just be careful you

don't get shot by a drug dealer or stabbed by a hooker or worse! Buena-bloody-fortuna!"

Henri could not believe it. He felt the goosebumps spring out all over his skin and cold thrill run down his spine. Buenafortuna, in the country where his great grandfather Li-Han had run his bar and brothel; the land where his grandfather, for whom he was named, had become a wealthy businessman; and where his poor father Pascal had been born only to be deported before he was two months old. *This must be Fate*, Henri reasoned and went to bed certain that his fortune was finally secured and that his ship was literally, about to come in.

The next morning, shortly after dawn, the *Spirit of Colchis*, aided by a slightly tipsy harbour pilot, clunked its rusty soon-to-be carcass against the dock of Buenafortuna and for the third time in four generations, a Cheung stepped onto this tropical soil ten thousand miles from Hong Kong.

With a little over eight thousand dollars in his pocket, his head full of dreams of making good and his unshakeable belief in his own talents and abilities, Henri Cheung could feel success in his bones. And for the first time in his life, he exercised a little self-discipline. Instead of heading to the capital with its casinos and bordellos and opportunities for easy money soon lost, Henri bought an old motorbike and armed with his six-month visa (purchased unofficially at the harbour for four hundred dollars which was fifty more than he paid for the motorcycle) he set off to find the perfect spot to make his fortune. He spent the next three months criss-crossing the provinces in search of the ideal place to set up. He even visited the little failed Belgian colony of San Cristobal to pay his respects to his great-grandfather's enterprising spirit. When the Belgians left, the town had been renamed Independencia but by now it was practically deserted and overgrown as the jungle reclaimed its former realm. Henri didn't really have an exact idea of what he would do but he knew it would be retail of some sort. His only plan was to find somewhere fairly remote where whatever he did would be a certain monopoly. So, he avoided the growing coastal cities and the large provincial centres, and one blisteringly hot December lunchtime he pulled into a filling station with one lonely pump on the edge of a large village. San Juan consisted of perhaps two hundred single-storey white plaster houses with corrugated iron roofs; a handful of more imposing two-storey brick houses; dusty streets full of stray dogs; barefoot children kicking an old football around; mothers with babies gossiping outside the laundrette; rusty pick-up trucks full of old tyres and scrap metal; five bars; one restaurant; a police station, which looked boarded up and abandoned; a town hall which doubled up as the school; and a place where no one seemed in a hurry and even the flies were too lazy to be much of a nuisance. In fact, there were only two real employers in the town, a beer-bottling plant some two miles away and a stone quarry that was five miles beyond the village and had its own small fleet of buses to ferry the workers to and fro. While Henri was waiting for some sign of life from the garage, he wandered down the only paved road in San Juan which ran for about five hundred yards through the middle of town and looked at the few shops: an ironmonger, a bakery, a hairdresser, a kiosk selling newspapers, a small bank, two tiny, under-stocked general stores (a third general store was closed and looked as if it had been for a while) and the little filling station whose owner emerged from his booth yawning and scratching his behind through his overalls.

Henri filled his tank but left the bike at the garage and returned to the centre of San Juan and into a bar with iron grilles on the windows. It was a dark and dingy cantina, lit by a single naked lightbulb swinging softly in the slight waft created by the three-bladed ceiling fan that provided no relief from the oppressive heat. There were four old men in the bar, sitting on deckchairs at a wooden table playing cards and each was nursing a rapidly warming bottle of beer and occasionally exchanging a word with the unshaven barman dressed in paint-spattered jeans and a grubby white vest. A radio was producing a tinny salsa in the background and Henri half expected it to stop as he walked in like the piano at a Wild West saloon. In fact, he was rather disappointed that the old men barely looked up from their game and the rough-looking, unkempt barman, who introduced himself as Paco, asked him very politely what he could get him. Two hours later, Henri emerged from the bar, blinking in the fierce sunlight and several dollars lighter having stood a few rounds of drinks and let himself be 'taken' at a few hands of cards. He had a hint of a smile on his face and his eyes were shining. He had found his El Dorado.

Within three months of that first morning in San Juan, Henri had been quick to act. His two-hour chat in the bar had yielded him with the information he needed about the local population, the neighbouring villages, the proximity of the nearest large town and shopping centres and the amenability of the local mayor and police to unofficial welfare contributions. He rented an empty two-room shack from the bar owner and then took a week to go to the capital, call his uncles and aunts and apply for temporary residency. His family wired him an additional fifteen thousand dollars over four days and he gained a four-year-residency permit from the Immigration Department and all it cost him was a bottle of Chanel perfume and a swing set for the daughter of the chief of the residency department. Before he left the capital, he went to one of the major distributors for the grocery sector; a few notes and the odd bottle of Johnny Walker black label changed hands and all was set.

Arriving back in San Juan, Henri leased the disused general store, which he planned to convert into his home, and then went to visit the owners of the two other general stores in town. As it turned out, they were owned by the same family: headed by Carlos Lopez; assisted by his wife, Nora; two sons who worked in the quarry but helped out when they could; and three daughters, sixteen-year-old twins, Maria and Marta who were fat, jolly and always singing along to American pop songs blaring out from an old cassette player, and Constanza, a pretty girl, able and quick-witted. However, at twenty-six years old, Constanza was still single and rather than admired for her strength and brains was pitied by the population of San Juan as she was unmarried and childless. Henri introduced himself to Carlos Lopez and within a month, Carlos, Nora and the twins left town in a rusty blue Hilux bound for a new life running Nora's ageing parents' lemon farm some seventy miles away, and with Henri's help, the boys were offered their own little house in the tiny village that was just being built at the quarry. That left Constanza in the Lopez family home and manager of one of the general stores and Henri as manager of the other and owner of both. Three months after that and Henri gave up the lease on the disused store and was living with Constanza in her family home. Henri sold both the remaining stores and had two twenty-foot containers shipped in and placed just behind the filling station as he reasoned it was strategically better placed to catch whatever passing trade there might be, however meagre, and as it was only a couple of hundred yards from the main street, and now the only general store in town, the local residents would learn to live with the minor inconvenience.

Within a year, Constanza was expecting Henri's baby and although they hadn't bothered getting married, they were happy and their business, the Angel Mart, was thriving because it was a virtual monopoly. More than that, because Henri was a wizard at getting just about anything that anyone needed and Constanza was so hard-working; and since the two of them were careful to be generous to the local school and the mayor's fundraising efforts to bring a clinic to town and they regularly gave out little candies and gum to the neighbourhood children, Angel Mart was turning an decent profit. The only fly in this rather pleasant ointment was the visits Henri occasionally had to pay to the capital to organise resupplies or to keep his immigration officer sweet. Constanza didn't mind the absences but she did worry that Henri might spend time and money in the casino. He had told her a little of his past and to Constanza, it seemed she should be more worried about Henri's gambling rather than womanising. In fact, she was right, Henri loved to flirt but since meeting Constanza, he was more than content to leave other women alone but it was true, he did visit the casinos in the capital and although he was not reckless, he steadily lost more than he won and once little Clara was born during a torrential rainstorm one April, Constanza confronted Henri and he was put on official warning about his love of games of chance.

A few years passed and Henri and Constanza made a considerable success of the Angel Mart and Henri was able to pay back his family but although with Clara they had a comfortable life, there was never much spare cash at the end of the month because Henri was still not fully cured of his gambling. Clara was growing into a chatty, lively girl who spoke Spanish and Cantonese with easy charm and was her parent's pride and joy.

All was well until Henri's latest trip to the capital to renew his rolling residency. This time, he stayed away from the casinos but on arriving at the Immigration Department, to his dismay he found that his usual amenable contact was away on extended sick leave and try as he might, the replacement section chief was not a man to be encouraged financially or through flattery to assist in Henri's residency renewal without a full police background check. In fact, it was worse than that, the section chief insisted that if Henri wanted to stay in the country (since he and Constanza were not married, he could not claim a spouse visa – Henri swore he would marry her as soon as he got back to San Juan), he would have to return to Hong Kong and apply through the consulate there and obtain his police report locally. Henri groaned. Although it would be nice to see his father and his family again, he did not want to leave Constanza, Clara and the Angel Mart and he couldn't take his family with him and just close up for however long the bureaucracy would take.

Talking it over with Constanza that evening, Henri heard two things from Constanza that he was not expecting: the first was that she would not marry him until he sorted his residency out and gave up gambling for good. The second was that she thought he should invite his father, Pascal over to stay with her and Clara while Henri returned to Hong Kong to sort his paperwork out. Constanza reckoned that it would be lovely for Clara to meet her grandfather and for her to meet her de facto father-in-law for the first time. It would also be an extra pair of hands in the Angel Mart and Clara could interpret for Pascal and it would also give the old man a chance to see the land of his birth.

When Henri arrived in Hong Kong he spent the first three days in a social whirl visiting friends and family and spending time with Pascal who was overjoyed at the prospect of flying out to see his granddaughter and of being some use to his son. Father and son went to the consulate to visit Sr Canto, the visa officer and that is where there was bad news and good news: the bad news was Henri, having come to an accommodation with Sr Canto regarding his lack of police certificate, did not want to approach his family for this financial accommodation as he had led them to believe that all was in order. However, he found himself with just a thousand dollars in his pockets since Constanza had insisted he leave all the rest of his cash with her. The good news was that, although deported when just a few weeks old, the years had seen revisions in the constitution and, ironically, Pascal was granted permanent leave to remain in the land where he was born. So, Pascal left Henri to his various money-making schemes in Hong Kong and the meeting at the airport with Constanza and Clara was appropriately touching with just the right combination of tears and laughter.

And while Henri sweated away trying to come up with the cash and paperwork needed for the meticulous and unscrupulous Sr Canto, Constanza ran the Angel Mart and Pascal chattered away to Clara and made her a beautiful wooden doll's house and rocking horse. He also had time to start his magical, surreal carvings again and an occasional passer-by would stop and look and one or two even offered to buy a piece of two but Pascal just smiled a smile of non-comprehension, shrugged apologetically and carried on carving. Pascal would help with the shelf stacking in the mornings and play with Clara in the afternoons while Constanza was busy in the shop, and he enjoyed cooking in the evenings while Constanza did the books or read to Clara and they would talk about Hong Kong with nine-year-old Clara interpreting, both adults marvelling at the easy manner in which she happily chirped away in two such different languages.

About a month after Pascal arrived, there was still no sign of Henri's immediate return and supplies were running low in the Angel Mart since Henri had not paid the distributer his usual 'handling fee; and Constanza was getting worried. So, one morning, she decided that action was needed and taking a bundle of cash, she headed for the bus stop for the four-hour journey to the capital to arrange for resupplies. She would be gone overnight and was happy to close up for the day and leave Pascal to keep an eye on Clara. But Pascal would hear none of it. He insisted that he could keep an eye on the shop and Clara (who was on her summer holidays) and make sure Angel Mart stayed open and earning. So, reluctantly, Constanza kissed her daughter, embraced Pascal and set off for the bus.

It was seven-thirty in the morning. Two hours later, poor Pascal was enduring the verbal onslaught from the angry customers outside the Angel Mart and Clara was doing her nine-year-old best to keep the ship afloat while Pascal floundered and flustered and wished he had never had the idea to open the shop.

Denis Ryan was drunk. Not even hungover, just still plain drunk from the night before. He had been out in Santa Cruz and Matthew had left him in some tequila bar in the company of a retired marine colonel and a couple of local hookers and they had stayed up and drank and smoked a few joints until the sun was almost up. Now, at a little after seven in the morning, Denis was awoken by the phone ringing in his hotel room, Denis was dry-mouthed and light-headed and the voice on the other end of the phone seemed to scream at him.

"Hey, Den, it's Matt. Had a good night?"

"Hmm, oh Matt, yeah, yeah, great. You OK?"

"Fine, friend! Listen you go ahead and rest, I am going off for a wander about today and I'll see you back in the bar at say, seven?"

"You going to be ok?"

"I am a thirty-seven-year-old Oscar-nominated movie star who has played a special-forces hero, a cowboy and a super-hero from Alpha Centauri, I think I can manage a day driving a jeep around the countryside without getting into too much trouble! Besides, I want to get a feel for the places you checked out to see if they fit in with the script."

"OK, have fun and don't get lost! The studio will kill me if I lose their multi-million-dollar-spinning leading man!"

"Sure thing, Den! See ya!"

Duel in the Dust was to be a modern Western and represented a personal crusade for Matt Marshall who over the last seven years had established himself as one of Hollywood's more thoughtful leading men. Born Matthew McKinley in Dundee, Scotland, Marshall had a degree in fine arts from the University of Edinburgh and had only got into acting when his girlfriend at the time, Sandy, was in an amateur production of *Cat on a Hot Tin Roof* playing Maggie. The actor playing Brick got food poisoning the night of the dress rehearsal and the understudy was too scared to go on. Matt had been at most of the rehearsals and had read through the lines with Sandy and, in desperation, the director asked whether Matthew would step in. He agreed and the play was a great success. Matthew was a big hit with his charismatic performance and rugged Celtic good looks and Sandy told him he was destined for great things.

Several years later and after some touring in rep and a couple of parts in TV dramas in UK, Matthew McKinley, now Matt Marshall was the newest brooding heartthrob in Tinsel Town. Oscar-nominated and winner of several newcomer awards, he was on that starry celebrity wave but Matt was not a party animal and lived quietly in the Hollywood hills and chose his parts carefully, directed a couple of independent movies and painted and collected small but exquisite pieces of art. He even put the money up to open a tiny gallery on Rodeo Drive to showcase new artists, particularly from Native American or Inuit backgrounds.

His latest project, *Duel in the Dust* was one he was very passionate about. He had written the screenplay himself and was set to direct. The *Duel* was not a shoot 'em up action movie. It was about a man's search for his missing wife and the duel was with his conscience and memories of how she had come to be missing. Having cast around for a suitable location to start filming, Denis Ryan, who was not only a good friend but also one of the leading location managers in the movies, had called excitedly one evening to say he had found the perfect place to shoot the movie. Arid and dusty with an unforgiving interior, spectacular coastlines, rich jungle vegetation and one-horse towns all within a single lonely province on the Pacific coast and in a country where labour was cheap and the local governor said he would put his entire staff and police at the crew's disposal in return for a small part in the film.

Matt and Denis had flown down from LA to Mexico City then taken a small commercial jet on a two-hour flight, then a much smaller single prop plane to a dusty strip cut out of the thorny scrubland about twelve miles from Santa Cruz, and had rented an old Jeep to explore the terrain. Although offered a brand new Ford Explorer by the Governor who came to meet them in person at the landing strip, Matthew preferred to 'go native' and experience the land without air conditioning, electric seats or Bose CD player. Denis knew his friend well enough not to complain. Besides, the Governor himself loaded a cooler full of the delicious golden local beer into the back of the jeep.

And it was in this old white jeep with no roof and mismatched tires, with a crackly salsa blaring out of the radio that Matt Marshall set off to explore the area surrounding Santa Cruz and after a couple of hours with an overheating radiator, pulled into the lonely filling station in San Juan.

Luckily for Matt, the garage attendant was there even though the gas station was usually closed on Sundays as he needed to get some petrol for his own car. Using gestures and cursing his ignorance of foreign languages (Matt knew a little Italian from his studies in Renaissance art and spoke schoolboy French but that was about it) and handing over three-twenty dollar bills to Sr Martino, Matt left the car in the care of the fortunate garage owner and wandered off to find a cold drink.

Just behind the garage was a long low metal building looking for all the world like a couple of shipping containers bolted together and painted in Coca-Cola red and white livery. Gathered around a raised hatch was a small crowd of local men and women all of whom seemed to be angry and directing that anger through the hatch. Being over six feet tall, Matt had no difficulty seeing over the heads of the vexed mob and peering into the dark recesses of the hatch, he saw a very flustered, old Chinese man gesturing and pointing to different products on the shelves behind him and looking as if he wanted the ground to open and swallow him up.

Just when it seemed that the mob were about to launch themselves through the hatch and drag the unfortunate Chinese pensioner out and vent their frustrations on him physically, a little girl with raven-black hair loose down to her waist and dark skin but with high cheekbones and sparkling brown almond shaped eyes came running around the corner, saying a few words in unmistakeable Chinese to the old man, she smiled sweetly and began talking to the small crowd in Spanish. Matt watched in fascination as the little girl conveyed the various requests for drinks and bread, cigarettes and eggs to what he supposed must have been her grandfather and the old man, relieved and cheerful again, busily gathered the needed items and chattered away merrily to the little girl.

Calm restored, Matt found himself alone with the little girl outside the hatch and the old man ducked inside the hatch then emerged, walking with a very heavy limp to stand beside them.

"Err… hola… un agua, por favor" Matt said using five of the twelve Spanish words he knew. The little girl didn't need to translate because the drinking from a bottle gesture that went with the request was evident to the Chinese man and he made to go back into the shop but the girl ran inside and a heartbeat later returned with an ice-cold bottle of water. Strangers were rare in San Juan and tall foreign ones even rarer and the little girl stood at her grandfather's side shyly looking at the new arrival. Matt smiled and took a five-dollar bill to hand to the little girl who took it and gestured for him to wait for his change.

"It's ok. Es bueno," Matt said indicating she should keep the change.

He was rewarded with a broad gap-toothed grin and a, "Gracias Señor," from the little girl and an equally broad and equally gap-toothed grin from the old man.

There is a moment each of us experiences when we make a sudden connection with someone irrespective of differences in gender, age, culture, language or location. It is perhaps some sort of empathetic chemistry when friendship and trust spontaneously appear and an immediate sense of comfort and companionship arise. Just such a moment now seemed to occur between Matt Marshall, the old and lame Chinese man and the pretty little girl by his side. Rather than taking his leave and heading back to get his car, Matt stayed and drank his water and sweeping his arm around in an arc and said, "Es bueno… mucho err… sol. Muy bella." He had no idea what he was saying really but he knew he wanted to stay a while and try to communicate. This village looked exactly the kind of place he had in mind for the opening scenes of *Duel*.

The little girl and the old man spoke together in Chinese for a moment then the little girl offering her hand and pointing at her chest said, "Soy Clara," then pointing to her grandfather, "Es mi abuelo, Pascal."

The old man placed his palm on his chest and, bowing slightly with his head, repeated, "Pascal."

Matt repeated the gesture and said, "Matt. Hola!"

Suddenly, Matt felt little Clara's hand slip into his own and she guided him away from the hatch followed by Pascal, who seemed to be protesting mildly, and around the corner.

Rounding the corner of the Angel Mart, Matt could see the small town with its white-painted houses and was already imagining where the opening shot would be filmed when feeling a tug on his hand he looked down and realised that Clara wanted him to look at something on her left.

He stared in amazement at around twenty pieces of carved wood, some finished in a high polish, others left in their natural state, but carving such as he had never seen before. They were all around two to three feet high and each piece was instantly recognisable as a bird, or a deer or a tree or something from nature but each piece also defied description as they were fashioned in beautiful, haunting shapes displaying a subtlety and emotion as if they were living embodiments of the carver's own soul not just his imagination. Matt was dumbstruck and moved with the sheer power of the pieces.

Clara, observing the deep impression the carvings had made on Matt, pointed to Pascal and then back at the carvings. Matt couldn't believe that this old Chinese man, who was actually blushing, was the creator of such incredible art.

"Es magnifico! I err... yo... quiero mucho!" Matt clumsily enthused. In fact, he had forgotten all about his overheating car, his drunken location manager and *Duel in the Dust* as he stood transfixed by the sheer beauty of the carvings. He had to take some pictures, this guy was a genius and the world needed to know. He had to get these pieces shown and his head was spinning with images of an exhibition in his gallery or in a Chinatown venue, of a book, of a documentary, of a million things and at the centre of it all, an unassuming, limping, gap-toothed old Chinese man with kind eyes and the heart and soul of a poet.

Clara could see that something strange was happening to Matt. She had seen it before as people, even the rather unsophisticated folk of San Juan fell under the spell of Pascal's carving and she was thrilled this tall foreigner was so impressed. Guessing he must be American, Clara had an idea. She ran into the shop and came back with a cheap cordless phone and pressed a few keys and a moment or two later was chatting excitedly to someone on the other end of the line.

It turned out that the sensitive and smart little girl

was calling her classmate, Eliza. Eliza was Clara's best friend but more importantly on a day like today, she was also the daughter of Helga. Helga was born in Denmark and her parents had brought her out when she was a teenager to follow her father's dream to open a chain of patisseries and upmarket bakers in the New World. Unfortunately, Helga's mother couldn't stand the heat and the dust and her father's plan never got further than a provincial bakery. After several years, her parents decided to return to Copenhagen but Helga, by then nineteen years old and in love with the local doctor's son wanted to stay. Her parents objected strongly, but Helga was determined and her fiancé, Maximo, was a kind, loving and devoted partner from a modest but respectable family and promised to look after her. Helga's parents reluctantly gave their blessing and left but came back to visit every couple of years and Helga did go back to Denmark once in a while. By the time Eliza was nine, Maximo was the only vet in the region and they owned one of the nicer two-storey brick houses in San Juan. Clara knew that Eliza's mother was foreign and therefore must be able to understand English and maybe she and Eliza would come over to help speak to the man. It was still not going to be easy; Helga had been deaf since she had meningitis when she was eleven. Before she became ill, Helga could speak five languages. As many Scandinavians do, she grew up knowing not only her native Danish but Swedish, Norwegian, German and English and she still read whatever books and magazines she could lay her hands on in English and she could read and write Spanish perfectly. Maximo and Eliza learned sign language and Helga worked as Maximo's veterinary nurse and was blissfully content with her family and her life in sleepy San Juan.

Clara ended her phone call with Eliza and signalled for a bemused Matt to wait and held up her hand with fingers splayed wide to show five minutes. Pascal and Matt lingered over the carvings and Matt ran his hands over the wood, which was warm and smooth to the touch and added to the seeming liquidity of the pieces. He was entranced and thrilled and felt a sense of childlike wonder.

Just under ten minutes later a white Toyota pick-up swung into view and an attractive, tall, blonde woman and an excited little girl, who looked very like Clara except for her grey eyes, emerged from the vehicle. The woman had a notepad and pen in her hand and the two little girls chattered away for a moment. Clara took Helga by the hand and led her over to where Matt and Pascal were standing. Matt was surprised that such a beautiful and clearly European woman was living in this little backwater but before he could say anything, Helga scribbled in the notepad and handed it to him.

"Hello. My name is Helga. I am Eliza's mother. I am sorry I cannot speak or hear but we can write notes and Clara tells me you have some questions for Pascal?"

Matt read the note and was touched that everyone was going to so much trouble. He nodded and smiled at Helga and mouthed a, "Thank you." Then taking the pen he paused because he didn't know where to begin. He had so many questions for Pascal, about his art about how he had come to live in San Juan and about his family and he had plenty of questions for Helga too. However, by way of experiment he jotted down a simple opening question.

"Did you do all of these carvings, Pascal?"

Helga read the question and signed to Eliza who asked the question in Spanish to Clara who in turn, asked the same question to Pascal in Chinese.

Pascal beamed and nodded and answered with a few sentences before Clara stopped him and turned to Eliza who was taking her task very seriously with her tongue between her teeth in concentration. Clara translated Pascal's answer into Spanish and the conscientious Eliza signed to her mother who wrote in the notepad in English and handed it again to Matt. As each person fulfilled their role the others watched them studiously and occasionally would burst into smiles and giggles and the long-winded process continued.

After the initial exchanges, it was clear it was going to be a long morning, so Pascal and Matt fetched a white plastic table from inside the shop and sitting on a few fold-away deckchairs with bottles of cold soda and water before them, Matt learned a little of Pascal's life with the delightfully enthusiastic help of two little girls and a beautiful Danish woman. Three hours later with the notepad full on both sides of the paper and the covers,

Matt Marshall took his leave promising to return soon with an interpreter and some books for Helga. Before he left, Matt begged Pascal to let him buy one of his pieces; it was in the form of a swan as if emerging from the water and the entire piece did indeed look as if it were moving and the fluidity was breath-taking. Matt opened his wallet and offered the entire contents to Pascal, which must have been about four hundred dollars. Pascal gently but insistently pushed the money back at Matt. Then saying a couple of words to Clara, Pascal stood back as the little girl picked up the carving which was almost as tall as she was and handed it to Matt.

"Un regalo de mi abuelo."

Matt did not need a translation and touching his heart with his hand he bowed at Pascal who bowed in return.

Although she didn't let on, Helga recognised Matt from the DVDs she occasionally bought that had subtitles and thought he was very handsome and not at all like a movie star, as she imagined. He was so gentle and kind and interested in everyone else and did not say a single thing about himself. Helga was looking forward to his next visit to San Juan and that night after Eliza was in bed, she cooked a big steak for Maximo and dragged him off before dessert for an early night. She adored her husband but allowed herself a little fantasy and Maximo was certainly not complaining.

Alfonso Dominguez was a vain, somewhat quick-tempered man. In his early fifties, short and stocky with a thick mop of black curly hair and strangely, rather feminine eyes, Alfonso was also kind, hard-working and rarely for this part of the world, enjoyed a reputation as both an honest and effective administrator of the province in which he had been placed in charge. Bereft of big cities or ports and with only a small cluster of coastal retirement towns in his domain, notably Santa Cruz, Alfonso was leader of the smallest and poorest province in the country but worked tirelessly to try and better the lot of its people. In the three years of his governorship, he had managed to bring electricity and clean water to every village between Santa Cruz and the border to the north, and a project was underway to achieve the same for the south. Alfonso, the son of a professional soldier and an opera singer, had been educated in the US and trained and worked as an attorney in the capital for twenty years, gaining a reputation for honesty which made his business suffer but when the post of governor of the forgotten province became vacant, President Dominguez (no relation) decided that the honest work-horse would be the ideal candidate to take charge of this impoverished poisoned chalice. Appealing to Alfonso's patriotism and his vanity, the President convinced him to take charge for an initial term of five years and promised he would have free rein in everything except taxation and the police. Alfonso agreed and within six months found himself working sixteen-hour days and travelling through the province in an official Ford Explorer with just his driver, Jorge, who doubled as the deputy governor. But Alfonso got things done. To raise extra money over and above the paltry central budget allowance, he had invited seven large companies in to build a range of plants from a canning factory to a massive recycling centre and construction was well under way on several others along with the necessary infrastructure. This not only provided jobs but allowed Alfonso to swell the provincial coffers by double. The reason the progress was so spectacular by local standards was that Alfonso Dominguez never took a penny for himself. His wife, Marisa came from one of the wealthiest families in Santa Elena and was as dedicated as her husband to the welfare of 'her' people. Together, they were a formidable team and it was no surprise that the President was outwardly fulsome in the praise he showered on his northern governor and privately fuming that this man might represent a popular challenge to his presidency one day. But that is another story...

The call from Hollywood had set the governor's mansion a-flutter. Alfonso could not only see the financial benefits to his province if he could get a major American studio to make a film here but also the potential for tourism and further cinematic adventures. A huge film fan, Alfonso felt he would be a good actor since he had spent his life performing either in the courts or in public meetings. So, he really pushed the boat out when it was confirmed that none other than Matt Marshall was coming to Santa Cruz with a colleague to scout out potential shooting locations. Alfonso went to meet them at the airstrip personally and offered them the use of one of the official cars but was a little taken aback to hear that Mr Marshall only wanted to rent some battered old peasant jeep. Still, Hollywood-types were a bit eccentric and Alfonso wanted to be a gracious and accommodating host.

A few days after the film star arrived, Alfonso was working in his office on a plan for a new irrigation system in the extreme south of the province when his secretary buzzed him on the intercom to announce that Sr Marshall was outside in the waiting area. Jumping up from his desk like an excited schoolboy, Alfonso ran to the door and flung it open and grasped Matt's outstretched hand with both of his and shook it vigorously and ushered the actor into his office with orders not to be disturbed.

Two hours later, Matt emerged from the office and went straight to the hotel to make a few calls while Governor Dominguez barked orders to all and sundry while juggling his desk telephone and two mobiles.

Two days later, San Juan experienced the arrival of a small convoy of four white and yellow official cars all bearing the crest of the province. The vehicles threw up clouds of dust and pulled into the filling station in front of the Angel Mart. People came out of houses and shops to join others standing in the street to stare at this unusual sight. Presently, out of the first car stepped the Governor and Matt Marshall, soon to be joined from the other cars by Denis Ryan, who immediately started looking around with his fingers in front of his face framing imaginary shots, an oriental looking woman in a very formal business suit and a young blond man with the bluest eyes anyone in San Juan had ever seen.

Waiting to meet the new arrivals were Pascal and Clara, Eliza and Helga and Helga's husband Maximo, who was on his way to vaccinate some cattle but was equally excited to meet a real film star. In front of them all standing protectively was Constanza. She had heard about the events in San Juan the day she went to the capital for supplies and was concerned and excited at the same time.

Pascal and Matt greeted each other like old friends and Matt gave a hug and kiss on the cheek to the girls including Helga who, remembering her fantasy, blushed deeply. Maximo introduced himself in broken English then kissing his wife rather more passionately than usual in public, he got in his pick-up and drove off to his next call. Matt politely greeted Constanza and the formally dressed oriental lady who introduced herself as Ann Lee of the Taiwanese trade delegation and who spoke impeccable English, Spanish and Cantonese acted as interpreter. The tall blonde foreigner with the china-blue eyes then stepped forward with a large duffle bag. Setting the bag down before Helga's feet, he started to sign to her. Helga laughed and cried at the same time and threw her arms around the young man and then did the same to Matt. Per Carlsson was the son of the Swedish ambassador who had come out to teach special needs children in a Swedish charitable initiative. Per could not only speak perfect English and Danish but had also learned to sign. The duffle bag was full to bursting with books and DVDs in English, Danish and Swedish and included several of Matt Marshall's films, which embarrassed Matt deeply.

The Governor who was unused to not being the centre of attention allowed these pleasantries to continue for a few minutes before clearing his throat and immediately commanding the scene. In fact, Alfonso was enjoying watching these people delight in each other's company but he felt he ought to give Matt a display of his skills as a sort of unspoken audition for a part in the upcoming film. As it turned out, Alfonso Dominguez did have a small part in *Duel in the Dust* and this would not be his only appearance on the big screen.

Going up to Constanza, he introduced himself and asked her as acting head of the family, if she would be willing to travel to Santa Cruz with her father-in-law, daughter and friends for a special meeting to organise a trip to Los Angeles for them all to see Pascal's work exhibited in Matt Marshall's gallery. Constanza was speechless and while the girls jumped up and down in excitement and Miss Lee translated for Pascal who didn't know where to put himself, the Governor explained that she need not worry about closing Angel Mart as he would personally ensure that there would be someone trustworthy to run the town's only shop for a couple of days while they were in Santa Cruz making arrangements. Constanza thanked the Governor and said she would be honoured then very shyly and almost inaudibly added that Pascal wasn't her father-in-law strictly speaking as she and his son Henri had never got round to getting married.

Alfonso laughed and hugging Constanza round the shoulder he whispered in her ear, "Actually, Senora, my parents never married either!"

The little group spent the next hour chatting and marvelling at Pascal's carvings and Pascal presented the Governor with a beautiful piece reminiscent of a jaguar but yet strangely human too. The Governor was deeply moved and felt humble to be in the presence of such a genius. Pascal scratched his head as he was sure the interpreter had got it wrong and he could not understand why everyone was so excited about his hobby.

Shooting started on *Duel in the Dust* about ten months after that morning in San Juan, long after the rains and when the summer was at its most reliably hot and dry. The crew spent about six weeks in San Juan and two in and around Santa Cruz. Matt stayed at the Governor's mansion during the filming in Santa Cruz and in a huge silver trailer parked outside the Angel Mart the rest of the time.

Eliza, Clara, Constanza and about a dozen of the inhabitants of San Juan were all taking English lessons arranged by Matt at the studio's expense and Pascal was being taught Spanish by Miss Lee who took time off every week to come to San Juan with her fiancé, Enrique. And while Pascal practised his Spanish with the now much more informally dressed Miss Lee, Enrique who grew up on a cattle farm in New Mexico, would accompany Maximo on his rounds and then relax with a few beers. The film crew took over San Juan much to the overwhelming delight of the residents who organised a fiesta of welcome and several other fiestas for crew members' birthdays and any excuse they could think of. The chief organisers of these impromptu parties were Denis Ryan and his partner in crime and rum, Paco, the grubby-vest wearing innkeeper.

An odd little group of travellers left San Juan about six weeks before the film crew rode into town and took over. This curious little group, consisting of Constanza and Clara, Eliza and Helga and Pascal, were met at the Angel Mart by a white mini-bus on which Miss Lee and Denis Ryan were waiting and the party set off for the four-hour trip to the international airport and the week's only direct flight to Los Angeles. Matt Marshall had organised an exhibition of Pascal Cheung's carvings and using all the undeserved clout of his celebrity status had tracked down the majority of Pascal's brothers and sisters and nieces and nephews and flown them over for a family reunion in California. Pascal remained in a daze throughout the entire experience and when Matt told him, via Miss Lee, that one of his pieces, the 'Dragon in the Sun' had sold for $200,000, the old man fainted and had to be revived with Jasmine tea laced with a little whiskey. In all, the exhibition which displayed twenty-six of Pascal's carvings, of which seven were for sale (the rest

Pascal gave to his relatives as gifts), raised a little under $500,000. Pascal kept $20,000 for himself for wood and some new tools and gave the rest to Constanza who, in consultation with Matt's financial wizards, decided to put half of it into a trust fund for Clara's future and used the rest to build a lovely two-storey brick house in San Juan, to buy a nearly new Hyundai and to extend the Angel Mart (by way of another container) and install air-conditioning inside. After all of this and other expenses for restocking the shop and donating money to the school for a permanent English teacher (her donation was matched by Alfonso out of his own pocket), there were a few thousand dollars left which she knew how she was going to spend.

During the exhibition in Los Angeles, Angel Mart had remained open. The store was left in the capable hands of its founder and owner, Henri. This Henri was somewhat chastened but relieved and delighted not only to be back in San Juan in his cherished Angel Mart but also to be back with his beloved and ultimately forgiving Constanza, his darling daughter, Clara and his now celebrated father, Pascal.

A couple of months after that first meeting between Matt and Pascal in San Juan, Constanza summoned up the courage to call the office of the Governor. It took several days and hours of waiting to be connected but finally, Alfonso Dominguez was on the line. Their conversation lasted about twenty minutes. A day after that, Sr Canto, the visa officer at the consulate in Hong

Kong received a call from home. Twenty minutes after this, Henri got a call on one of the mobiles in his cab from Sr Canto. Two days after that, Henri boarded a flight to Los Angeles with an onward booking for home.

When he arrived back in San Juan, Pascal and Clara were not around but Constanza was there, standing outside the Angel Mart rather than wait for him at home. Henri had been gone three months and things had definitely changed. He had missed his family and his home so much that Henri had determined to stop gambling and be a better partner and father, and that he would work hard to earn Constanza's consent to marry him, not for the passport, but because he loved her and he wanted to show the world how much.

Constanza kissed him and just said, "It's good to have you home, Henri. Now, let's just be a family, ok?"

The wedding took place during a break in filming and San Juan had never seen anything like it. The Governor and his wife were there as well as an assortment of Hollywood actors and actresses and the entire town of San Juan turned out.

Pascal had been working in secret on a special gift and only Clara knew what it was as it had been her little bit of gossip that had inspired him. The gift caused a gasp of joy in Constanza and fairly knocked the legs from under Henri… it was a crib.

Six months later, Constanza Cheung as she now was, gave birth to a little boy. She named him Lionel. The first syllable of the name was in honour of his great-

great grandfather, the first Cheung to find himself in this strange and wonderful land, Li-Han.

Henri, Constanza, Clara and little Lionel went off to visit Constanza's parents for a couple of days to introduce them to their new grandson. They left the shop open at Pascal's insistence and by now his Spanish was just about sufficient to reduce the amount of angry shouting and gesturing at the hatch of the Angel Mart to no more than a few huffs and puffs and the occasional stamp in the dust.